Hello!

This is Kat's story. She lov
friends and her infuriating
but she wishes her parents w
stop treating her like a little girl!

Like Kat, when I was a teenager I was
impatient to grow up. I wanted to
explore the world and have adventures.
And I did! I visited lots of amazing
places. I swam with dolphins in New
Zealand, walked in a whispering bamboo
forest in Japan and kayaked through
mangroves sprinkled with glow worms in Thailand.

But the most magical place I have ever visited was a tiny
island in Sweden.

My brother, sister and I stayed with a friend, Jakob, and one day he
took us out on his boat to a deserted island. It was covered in wild
flowers, bees and rocks, and surrounded by a dark blue sea that
sparkled in the sun and stretched for miles. First, we ran all over the
island screaming (because having your own island for the day is
exciting), then we had a picnic. Next, we decided to go for a swim.
We were still changing when Jakob ripped off his T-shirt, leapt into
the sea, swam to a cliff, climbed it, then – without hesitating – dived
straight back into the sea.

Wow, I thought. I would love to do that . . . but I didn't.

I never forgot the adventure of visiting that beautiful island and now, in
Sunkissed, Kat is going back there. Turn the page and discover what
happens when one girl is brave enough to take the plunge and jump
into the unknown.

Jenny x

Also by **JENNY McLACHLAN**

FLIRTY DANCING
LOVE BOMB

ABOUT THE AUTHOR

Before Jenny started writing books about the Ladybirds (Bea, Betty, Kat and Pearl), she was an English teacher at a large secondary school. Although she loved teaching funny teenagers (and stealing the things they said and putting them in her books), she now gets to write about them full-time. When Jenny isn't thinking about stories, writing stories or eating cake, she enjoys jiving and running around the South Downs. Jenny lives by the seaside with her husband and two small but fierce girls.

Twitter: @JennyMcLachlan1
Instagram: jennymclachlan_writer
www.jennymclachlan.com

SUN KISSED

JENNY McLACHLAN

BLOOMSBURY
LONDON OXFORD NEW YORK NEW DELHI SYDNEY

Bloomsbury Publishing, London, Oxford, New York, New Delhi and Sydney

First published in Great Britain in August 2015 by Bloomsbury Publishing Plc
50 Bedford Square, London WC1B 3DP

www.bloomsbury.com

Bloomsbury is a registered trademark of Bloomsbury Publishing Plc

A CIP catalogue record for this book is available from the British Library

ISBN 978 1 4088 5611 6

Typeset by RefineCatch Limited, Bungay, Suffolk
Printed and bound in Great Britain by CPI Group (UK) Ltd, Croydon CR0 4YY

1 3 5 7 9 10 8 6 4 2

For Ben, who means the world to me.

ONE

I'm hiding in my bedroom wardrobe with my sister's ex-boyfriend. This might be the worst decision I've ever made in my life.

Downstairs, my family are crashing around. Dad's banging pans and saying 'spaghetti bolognaise' in a shocking Italian accent, Britta's practising her piano scales and Mum's slamming doors and yelling, 'Kat, Kat!'

'Why are we hiding?' whispers Joel.

'Shhh!' I say, then I listen as Mum comes up the stairs and starts looking for me. Through the slats in the wardrobe door, I see her glance into my room. Then she calls out, 'I can't find her anywhere.'

'Spaghetti bolognaise!' replies Dad, and I hear his heavy footsteps on the stairs. Oh no. I've got a terrible feeling about this.

Next to me, Joel starts to wriggle. 'Keep still,' I hiss. 'Dad gets well scary when he loses his temper.' Joel freezes just as Dad strides into my room. He stands on my rug with his hands in the pockets of his hideous running shorts – the ones cut high at the sides to show a lot of hairy thigh. He's just worn them to Britta's parents' evening. How could he?

I hold my breath and try to make myself as small as possible. Dad turns in a circle, his eyes narrowed, and for a moment he seems to stare straight at me. Then I see Pinky step into my room. Dad looks at her and frowns as she rubs against his leg. He doesn't stroke her. Pinky happens to be hairless after a fight with a fox and no one really enjoys touching her. She steps lightly away from Dad, walks towards the wardrobe door and starts sniffing the slats. *Go away, Pinky!* Just when I think Dad's going to stomp over and pull open the door,

Mum shouts, 'Check the garden,' and he walks out of my room.

I let out my breath. I'm such an idiot! Why didn't I just put Joel in the wardrobe? I didn't need to get in with him: I'm supposed to be in my bedroom! Next to me, Joel shifts around and whispers, 'Maybe we should –'

'Shh!' I say. 'He might come back.' We sit in silence for a few moments. 'OK. He's gone, so I'm going to go downstairs and I'll come and get you when it's safe for you to leave. You'll have to wait until everyone goes to bed.'

'But I told my mum I'd walk the dog.' I stare at Joel's shadowy face. I don't remember his voice being so whiney when he was going out with Britta. I must have zoned it out and focused on his superb grooming. Problem is, in the dark I can't see his gorgeous hair, but I can hear his voice.

'Can't you walk him later?'

'He's got irritable bowel syndrome. It's not good if he doesn't get regular walks . . .' Joel's breath is warm on my cheek and smells of chocolate cupcakes. When he turned up this evening asking for Britta – looking like a model in his tight Levi's shirt – I told him to come in and wait for her. Then I gave him a cupcake, and then I asked him if he wanted to listen to some music up in my room, and that's how we ended up in the wardrobe. Right now, he's panting sugar on my face and I'm finding it hard to breathe.

'Joel,' I say, leaning away from him, 'you do under-stand that if Mum and Dad catch you in here I am *dead*?'

'Because I'm a boy?'

'Yes, because you're a boy . . . who went out with my sister. Plus, you're eighteen and I'm fifteen. Also, I've done some things recently that they aren't too happy about.'

'Like what?'

'A couple of times I skived off school during PE. Which was fine, until our neighbour saw me sunbathing on the grass outside Tesco's and told Mum. I said I'd

4

rather get a tan than be stuck indoors playing ping-pong, which Mum kind of understood, but then there was the shoplifting incident.'

'You shoplifted?' Joel's squeaky voice goes up a notch.

'Only a smoothie, and I lost Mum's handbag.'

'Wow! Britta always said you were –'

'What?'

'Well, doing stupid stuff.'

My sister is such a cow. 'It wasn't as bad as it sounds,' I say, pulling a stiletto out from under my bum. 'Stealing the smoothie was an accident. I ran out of Marks and Spencer's when I realised I'd left Mum's Prada bag in a changing room and I forgot to pay for the smoothie.'

'Prada sounds expensive.'

'It was, hundreds of pounds expensive. It was her fortieth birthday present from my dad.' I remember Mum's face when she collected me from Marks and Spencer's and how she cried in the car on the way home.

Not about the handbag. She said it was seeing me sitting in the manager's office 'like a criminal'. When I asked if we could stop at the drive-through McDonald's to get a milkshake – they wouldn't let me keep the smoothie – she *freaked*.

After a moment's silence, Joel says, 'I don't think you're stupid, Kat. Actually, I really like you.'

'What?' I whisper.

'I like you. I even liked you when I was going out with Britta.'

I sit in stunned silence. Wow. There is just so much wrong with that. Now I'm really worried about Mum and Dad finding him in here! Joel shuffles round so our faces are centimetres apart. I try to back away, but there's nowhere to go.

This is all Britta's fault. When they left for her parents' evening, Mum said, 'Fingers crossed the teachers say nicer things than they did about Kat!' And they all laughed because Britta's a genius, so obviously they'll say better stuff about her. I'm the opposite

6

of a genius. I'm the smoothie thief. When I saw Joel standing on the doorstep, I invited him in to teach my family a lesson. I wasn't sure what the lesson was going to be, I just knew it would annoy them to find Joel in my room. But the moment I heard Britta yell, 'We're back!' I knew I'd made a terrible mistake, which is how we ended up in here.

In the darkness, Joel finds my hand and squeezes it. 'And I mean, I *really* like you . . .'

'Oh,' I say, and I gulp, but maybe it sounds like, 'Mmm,' because he puts his arm round me and starts rubbing his nose in my hair. I've got to get out of here! I fumble through dresses and jumpers, trying to get my fingers in the gap in the door, but as I lean forward, he starts *kissing* me.

Actually, he's kissing my ear.

Does this count as a kiss? If it does, it's my third-ever kiss. Joel's ear-kiss is moist and gross. Part of me wants it to stop immediately, but a bigger part of me knows this is going to be a really funny story to tell my

7

friends because I'm fairly certain Joel thinks he's kissing my mouth.

Suddenly, Joel breathes out and it's so tickly I burst out laughing. Next, footsteps crash across my room, my wardrobe door is thrown open and I tumble on to the carpet. Joel and some shoeboxes land on top of me.

I stare up at Dad, blinking into the bright light. 'Sorry, sorry!' says Joel as he desperately tries to untangle his shirt button from my hair. Then Pinky strolls in, followed by Mum and Britta. Pinky starts to bite my toes, Britta gasps and covers her mouth, but Mum doesn't even look surprised. She just shakes her head and says, 'Oh, Kat, how could you?' which is word for word what she said at Marks and Spencer's.

And then I make my second big mistake of the evening: I start to laugh . . . and I just can't stop.

One hour later, I've stopped laughing. Joel has gone – Dad chased him down the road, roaring, which can't have been a good experience – and I'm sitting in the middle of the sofa. Mum's curled up on the sheepskin beanbag biting her nails and Dad is pacing around the room. 'Your mother and I have been talking, Kat, and we've come to a decision.'

'*Mother?!*' I say, putting on a posh voice. 'Who's my *mother*?'

Dad stares at me and breathes deeply in and out through his nose. I stop grinning. 'As you have just demonstrated, you don't seem to take anything we say seriously and you don't appear to care for your sister's feelings –'

'Dad, that is *so* unfair. Britta dumped Joel over two months ago. He's up for grabs. A singleton. Those are the rules of dating . . .' The looks on their faces make me trail off.

'We know you're trying to be funny, Kat,' says Mum, 'but you really hurt Britta tonight.'

Ha, ha, ha! I laugh. Very quietly. In my head. Britta's the one who told her boyfriend I was stupid. As Mum stares at me, I think of all the times Britta's called me Dingbat, Dummy or, if Pinky's sitting on my lap, Dumb and Dumber. She even insults my cat, and Mum and Dad let her get away with it because they're always laughing along with her.

'So we've come to a decision about America.' Dad stops pacing and stands in front of me, his legs a metre apart. Hairs are literally crawling down his legs like they're trying to escape from his shorts.

'You should get a wax, Dad. *Seriously*, loads of men have them now.'

'We have come to a decision,' he says, ignoring me. 'We can't leave you here with Britta. Not for a whole month. It's not fair to expect her to look after a wild teenager.'

'What are you going to do with me, then?' Over the summer holidays, Dad's taking Mum with him on a business trip to the States. Apparently, this is their 'second honeymoon', but if I've added them all up right, it will be their 'seventh honeymoon'. Britta's supposed to be in charge, which basically means I get to do whatever I want for a month. But if they're not leaving me behind, then that must mean . . . 'Are you taking me with you?' I ask. 'Summer in Los Angeles . . . That would be awesome!'

'What?' says Dad, confused. 'No, of course we're not taking you with us. We've decided to send you to stay with Auntie –' I swear he pauses here, giving me a chance to run through all the terrible auntie options: Auntie Christie in Portsmouth, who wears leggings and crop tops, Auntie Joanna on the Isle of Wight, who's a witch (literally, it's her *job*), or Auntie . . .

'Frida,' says Mum, finishing his sentence. Frida, my Swedish auntie, who lives in Stockholm, and who loves nakedness.

'But,' I say, trying to work out what this will mean, 'I won't see my friends for the *whole* summer.'

'Well,' says Dad, arms folded, looking smug, 'you should have thought of that before you decided to get *intimate* with your sister's boyfriend.'

'He's her *ex*-boyfriend,' I mutter, but finally I decide to shut up. This is one serious punishment and unless I want to literally die of boredom, ABBA and pickled herring this summer, I need to get out of it *fast*.

TWO

'Look,' says Bea. 'A plane!'

Betty leans across my seat and the two of them peer out of the car window, watching as the plane flies low over the motorway. 'Betty, you're squashing me,' I say.

'Sorry.' She settles back into her seat. 'But did you see its little wheels come down? I've never been on a plane. This is so exciting!'

'Anyone want a yogurt raisin?' asks Bea, leaning forward and offering the packet to Mum and Dad. 'Or I've got Mini Cheddars.'

When my friends said they'd come to the airport to see me off, I didn't expect it to turn into such a fun day out for them. Mum takes a handful of raisins and starts feeding them to Dad. 'That was a Scandinavian Airlines plane, Kat. It could be the one you're going on.'

'Don't depress me, Mum.'

'Hey, girls,' Dad says, interrupting me. 'Don't you love this song?' Without waiting for a reply, he turns the radio up and starts to croon along to Adele singing 'Someone Like You'. Annoyingly, Bea and Betty join in, making Dad turn the music up even louder.

I sit back in my seat and try to control the sick feeling that is building up in my stomach. I can't believe Mum and Dad are actually doing this to me! I find flying scary, especially take-off, but knowing I'm not going to see my friends for a whole month is even worse than the thought of being thirty thousand feet in the air. Mum and Dad don't understand. They keep telling me I can speak to Bea and Betty on the phone and text, but I'll miss them so much.

A lorry overtakes us, spraying the window with grey water and making the car shake. It's been raining since we left our house, and now the car is steamed up. Betty's drawing a cartoon ghost on her window. She adds a speech bubble. Now the ghost is saying, 'Bye-bye!'

I must look sad because Bea nudges me. 'It's going to be alright, Kat.'

I'm not sure it is. In the front, I watch Dad rest his hand on Mum's thigh. 'Dad,' I say, '*please* don't perv on Mum in front of my friends!'

'Can't keep my hands off her.' He gives her leg a squeeze.

'I think your mum and dad are cute together,' whispers Bea. We watch as Mum puts her hand on top of Dad's and mashes it down into her leg. 'Oh,' says Bea. 'Less cute.'

'Seriously, you two, stop it. It's bad enough that I'm going to Sweden, without having to watch you two *make out* on the way to the airport.'

'If you hadn't been *making out* with your sister's boyfriend, you wouldn't be going to Sweden,' says Dad, glaring at me in the mirror.

'*Ex*-boyfriend,' I say wearily, 'and we weren't making out . . . at least, I wasn't.'

'Joel snogged Kat's ear,' says Betty. 'She didn't even like it. She said it felt like he was washing her ear out *with his tongue*!' Suddenly the car swerves as Dad lets go of Mum's leg and grips the steering wheel.

'Not really helping, Betty,' I say.

But she's not listening. 'Plane!' she shouts. 'I think I saw the pilot!'

'So,' says Dad, 'time to say our goodbyes?' I've checked in and we're standing by the electronic barriers that lead to security. Until now, Bea and Betty have been working hard to distract me. Betty even pushed me on a trolley all the way from the car park, pretending I was a giant baby. 'Your plane goes in just over an hour,' he adds, glancing at his phone.

So, it's actually happening. It was only when Mum started speaking to me in Swedish and a suitcase appeared in my room that I realised they were definitely

going ahead with the Auntie Frida plan. One suitcase . . .
one suitcase? I told Mum I needed three: one for clothes,
one for products and accessories, and one for technology, but she just laughed and said Frida's boat was too
small to take that much stuff.

'I don't want to go,' I say.

Mum and Dad exchange a look. We've been through
this so many times. Mum just keeps telling me how
much fun I'll have with Frida. I suppose she is pretty
cool. She's a jewellery designer and she lives on this
awesome houseboat in Stockholm, but without my
friends, Frida's boat will feel like prison. A prison with
loads of IKEA furniture and a guard who walks around
naked. 'Come here,' says Dad. 'Give your old man
a hug.'

'But who'll make Britta's breakfast smoothie? I'm
the only one who does it right. And there's no way she'll
water the plants.' He wraps his arms round me. 'Do I
have to go?' I ask, but he doesn't even answer my
question.

Next, I bury my face in Mum's grey cashmere shoulder. She smells of lemons. I don't want to let go because she's so soft. God, I wish she hadn't found the cardi in my suitcase and taken it out. All around us, people stream past, dragging trolleys and hyper children along with them. Except for me, everyone seems excited, like they're off on a big adventure. Over Mum's shoulder, Bea gives me a 'Be brave' smile and Betty sticks her tongue out and winks. The sight of Betty in her pink knitted hat makes me cling to Mum even tighter. She knitted it herself and although she claims it's a cupcake it looks much more like a boob. She really shouldn't have knitted a red cherry on the top.

'It's a question of trust, sweetheart,' Mum says, stroking my hair, 'and knowing you'll be sensible.'

'But, Mum, I am sensible.' She holds me at arm's length, taking in my playsuit and heeled boots, my tousled plait, beads and bangles. 'They're comfy boots, Mum. You should know. You're always borrowing them.'

'You look lovely,' she says, laughing. 'It's just not very practical for going on a plane.' *Or what Britta would wear*, I think. Even though she's only eighteen, she's always allowed to go off on her own, doing triathlons or camping with Venture Scouts. When she goes on a journey, she puts on a really ugly pair of cargo pants with loads of pockets that she stuffs full of plasters and baby wipes. They make her thighs look *enormous*.

'If you let me stay, I promise not to put any boys in my wardrobe.' This makes Betty grin and I nearly smile. 'I won't even put any clothes in there . . . or talk to any boys . . . or even *look* at boys. It's not like I had any massive parties planned.' I did. I had a monstrous sleepover planned for next Thursday.

'Kat hates boys and parties,' says Betty seriously, but then she ruins it by laughing madly and Bea joins in.

'Sorry,' says Bea, 'but it's funny because you *do* love parties and, well . . .'

'Boys?' I say.

'Yep.'

'I'm sorry, girls,' says Dad, 'but it's all arranged. We'll have a relaxing break and Kat will have a wonderful summer in Sweden.'

'Frida's mad. Don't make me live with her and her peasant clothes and her ambient music. Her boat rocks when cruise ships go past. I'll get seasick!'

'It's time to go,' says Dad firmly. Then he claps his hands together and says to my friends, 'Who's hungry? Anyone fancy sushi?'

'I've never eaten sushi,' says Betty.

'You'll love it,' says Dad, 'and I want some chicken katsu.'

I throw my arms around Bea and Betty for one last hug. 'You're not allowed any chicken katsu. It's my favourite. I'll be too jealous.'

'Definitely no chicken katsu,' says Bea.

'I fancy vegetable tempura,' says my mum, who's already looking around for a YO! Sushi, 'and maybe a cheeky glass of plum wine.'

'Mum, I haven't gone yet. Don't start celebrating.'

'Don't worry,' says Bea. 'Nothing happens in our town. You won't miss a thing.'

'You're not allowed to have any fun when I'm away. All you can do is hang out with your boring boyfriends and be boring.' For a moment, I'm struck by the total unfairness of Bea and Betty having boyfriends, while I – someone who has put a huge amount of effort into studying the opposite sex and looking awesome – have *never* been out with anyone. Not even for a day. Betty's wearing a knitted boob hat and she has a nice, normal boyfriend . . . and he's hot. *Really* unfair.

'Can we go to Brighton?' asks Bea.

'No.'

'The seaside? The fair? Lush?' she says.

'No, no and no!'

'What about KFC?' says Betty.

'OK. Just KFC.'

And then Dad holds my boarding pass up to the barrier, the doors slide open and, without realising what I'm doing, I step forward and the doors shut behind me. I can't stop and wave because immediately I'm moved on by a security officer.

'Place your belongings in here, please,' she says, passing me a plastic tray. I glance back; they're all walking away. 'Any liquids over one hundred millilitres?'

'How much is that?' I ask. She sighs and holds up a plastic bottle half filled with water. She swishes it from side to side. 'Um, maybe a couple of things,' I say. 'Perfume, moisturiser ... Does face-cooling mist count?' She narrows her eyes and nods. 'Coke?' I hold up my half-drunk bottle.

'I think you'd better open up your case.'

While the scary security lady rummages through my bag, I try to catch a last glimpse of Mum and Dad. They're disappearing round a corner, but Bea and Betty have hung back and are waving like mad, our Ladybird wave: thumb tucked in and four fingers wiggling.

We made up this wave at nursery school. There were four of us in the awesome Ladybird gang: me, Bea,

Betty and Pearl. I didn't ask Pearl along to the airport because Bea and Betty basically hate her. They've got pretty good reasons to hate her and I suppose I have too, but life is never boring when Pearl is around. I wiggle my fingers back at Bea and Betty. A sharp cough makes me turn round.

'What's this?'

'Serum,' I say. 'Loads of people think you can't use serum if you've got oily skin, but that's just not true. That's Clinique and it's very hydrating. You should try it. It's good on large pores.' It's dropped in the bin with a *clang* and a lump forms in my throat. Next she holds up my jar of peanut butter. 'No way!' I say. 'That's not a *liquid*.'

'No spreads, jams or preserves.' *Clunk*. In it goes.

When I turn back, they've disappeared. I search around for Betty's pink booby hat. Nothing. They've gone.

'Miss? Please step through the security archway.'

★

23

My plane is paused at the start of the runway, engines growling, moments away from take-off. I stare out of the rain-smeared window and try not to think about what's about to happen. I can't imagine how this huge plane, packed full of yelling children and holidaymakers, will ever get up in the air. It's not helping that the man next to me is holding his head in his hands.

The plane lurches forward and picks up speed. Suddenly, all I can think about is Pearl's text. I got it just before I turned my phone off: **Hope you don't die! Ha ha ha!!** We're bumping along faster now, and the pressure forces me back in my seat. The engines start to roar. I take deep breaths and grip my armrests. Faster. Faster. Then the nose of the plane tips up and, although it seems impossible, we are going up, up, up and we're in the sky!

'Oh, God,' moans the man next to me, who, incidentally, is wearing a vest when he clearly doesn't have the physique to wear a vest. If we crash, the last thing I'll see will be his skinny white arms. The plane banks dramatically to the left, and I look down at the sprawling airport, at the thousands of cars in the car park and at the motorway that curves like a river. Mum, Dad and my friends are down there somewhere, going home together, maybe singing along to Adele.

I press my fingers against the window and try to guess which tiny car is taking them further and further away from me.

THREE

'Kat! Kat! Kat!' Through the crowd of passengers, I see Auntie Frida coming towards me. She squeezes between an old lady sitting on a suitcase and a hugging couple. Frida's long embroidered dress and tangled hair look out of place in the modern airport. '*Hej!*' she says, pulling me to her for a hug. I'm squashed against her necklace, one of her own, a chain of silver acorns and twigs.

'Here you are,' she says, finally letting me go. Her face is clean and shiny and dusted with freckles. 'So your mum and dad have sent you to have some crazy fun with Auntie Frida?'

'I think the idea is you make sure I don't have any crazy fun.'

'Ha!' she cackles. 'We'll show them.' She takes my suitcase off me and heads for the exit. 'Come on, let's get out of here.' Stockholm airport is filled with light; sun streams in through the wall-to-ceiling windows and I can smell coffee and cakes – you can always smell coffee and cakes in Sweden. Frida darts ahead of me, almost at a skip, and that's when I notice she's not wearing any shoes.

I try to catch up with her. 'What's with the bare feet, Frida?'

'It connects me with the earth, you know?' She glances over her shoulder and smiles. 'When I go bare-foot, I feel like a goddess. You should try it!'

'No way.'

'Worried about treading in something?'

'No. I just love shoes,' I say.

This makes her laugh. 'Maybe a summer spent with me will change all that.'

'I don't know,' I say, struggling to keep up in my three-inch heels, 'I *really* love shoes.'

★

A few hours later, I'm sunbathing on the deck of Frida's boat, a coconut water in one hand and *Grazia* in the other. The sky is turquoise, dotted with clouds, and waves lap against the side of the boat, making my ice cubes clink. Stockholm's old town stretches in front of us, the houses painted a rainbow of colours. There's a blue-grey one I really like. I've been looking for a vest in that colour for ages.

Frida's sitting next to me, legs twisted into the lotus position, staring into space. 'I'm really into clouds at the moment, Kat. I've become a *cloud-spotter*.' She takes a sip of her drink. 'Look at that one.' She points up at the sky. 'It looks like . . .'

'Cotton wool?' I suggest. 'A sheep?'

'I was thinking, two seahorses kissing?'

'Yeah, maybe.' While Frida cloud-spots, I fashion-spot. 'Don't you love these earrings?' I turn round my magazine and hold it up for her. 'Hey, when can we go shopping? When I visited with Mum last year, we went to this shop where *all* the clothes were white.'

'Well, I guess we'll need to go soon, before the shops shut.'

'I can wait until tomorrow,' I say, suppressing the urge to jump up and start getting my stuff together.

'We're catching the early boat tomorrow. I want us to be on the first one that leaves for Stråla.'

'What?' I sit up and the Stockholm skyline wobbles. All this cloud-spotting and sun must have gone to my head. 'Where are we going tomorrow?'

'To Stråla, the island. I want to get the boat that leaves at eight.'

'We're going to an island tomorrow?'

'Didn't you know?' Frida puts down her drink. 'Kat, are you telling me your mum didn't mention Stråla?'

'Frida, I don't know what you're talking about.'

'Your mum is hopeless,' she says, laughing. 'Stråla is the most beautiful island in the world.' Her eyes widen. 'It's so peaceful. Totally isolated.'

'Isolated? How isolated?'

'It will take us over three hours to get there. It's miles out in the archipelago. One of the most distant islands.'

'Are there any shops?' I ask. If I'm honest, this is sounding like a pretty boring day trip.

'Sure! A wonderful village shop that sells *the best* cinnamon rolls.'

'Any cafes . . . restaurants . . . people?'

'One cafe and a few people,' says Frida, laughing, 'but you're going to love it, Kat. It's so relaxing. I went to stay there last year, and it *transformed* me. When I got back to Stockholm, I immediately booked the cabin for the whole summer.'

I drop my magazine on the deck and pull off my sunglasses. 'The *whole* summer?'

'That's right. The isolation fills me with creative energy. I'm going to keep making jewellery while I'm there.'

'But what about me, Frida? You do know I'm supposed to be staying with you for, like, *weeks*.'

'You will be staying with me . . . on Strála.'

'For a whole month?' I ask. I feel sweat breaking out on the back on my neck.

'That's right.' Her smile fades. 'I'm really surprised your mum and dad didn't tell you, Kat. They should have.'

'Yes,' I say. 'They should.' She reaches out for my hand. I feel sick. 'But what will I do all day?' I think back to family holidays we spent in the countryside in Sweden. 'Swim? Go for walks?'

'Exactly! Here.' She reaches into her bag and pulls out a creased brochure. 'I picked this up when I was there. You can read all about Stråla and get excited. It's going to be an adventure!'

On the front of the brochure is a photo showing the silhouette of a person standing on a rock, staring out to sea, the sun setting on the horizon. *Stråla: The Serene Isle*, I read. I flick through the pages. Mum and Dad knew Frida was spending her summer on Stråla and they tricked me into coming to Sweden just to get rid of me. I guess they thought they were being really clever sending me to a tiny, and presumably boy-free, island ... or maybe they didn't even give it a second thought.

What they've done to me is much, much worse than hiding a boy in your wardrobe.

'Looks good, doesn't it?' Frida's frowning. Already, I'm ruining her summer.

'Yes.' I look up from the images of sea, trees, cows and more sea. 'The brochure says we can "pick mushrooms" and "walk round the island to see sheep and cows".'

'We can't pick mushrooms because it's not the right season, but there will be lots of sheep and cows.'

'Great,' I say. I actually quite like mushrooms.

Frida stands up. 'Don't worry.' She pulls me to my feet. 'Let's go and get you shopped-out so you can't wait to get to Stråla tomorrow.'

Usually I love shopping and I particularly like getting ready to go, imagining the clothes I will see, the colours, the fabrics, the thought of finding something that's just perfect. But as I pull my dress on over my bikini and search around for my purse, I feel heavy. The thought of shopping always makes me happy. Why isn't it working today? I find my purse and check the credit card Mum gave me is in there. She said it was for 'emergencies'.

'Ready?' Frida's standing on the gangplank.

'Let's go,' I say, dropping my purse in my bag. *Guess what, Mum? I'm going to a tiny island for a month to look at cows*. I'd describe this as an emergency.

I can't sleep. Frida's boat is moored on a noisy quay lined with restaurants and bars. Laughter and music mix irritatingly with Frida's out-of-control wind chimes. Usually, I love falling asleep on her boat – it feels cosy – but tonight the shrieks of laughter keep making me jump. Also, it's *so* hot – apparently, it's the start of a heatwave – so I'm on top of my sheet, sweating in my pants and vest. I've opened the window as far as it'll go, but the air that's coming in is warm and smells of diesel.

Frida tried hard to give me a good evening. After some intense shopping, where I bought emergency high-waisted shorts, yellow sunglasses, lipgloss, water-resistant mascara, a straw hat and a troll key ring (for Betty), she took me to this elegant cafe full of girls who looked like models and men with trendy moustaches. So sweet. It wasn't her sort of place, but I loved it. We sat on the terrace on black-leather cubes, drinking iced tea. After a meal in a Thai restaurant we came back to the boat so Frida could finish packing.

Earlier, I tried to ring Mum and Dad, but their phones were turned off. I guess they're up in the air, flying to LA. Britta didn't answer either and I've just spent the past hour desperately messaging my friends. After I told them that Mum and Dad have sentenced me to a summer of acute boredom on Stråla, they've been trying to cheer me up. For example:

Betty: I bet Stråla will be packed full of HOT blond Scandi Gods eating meatballs and checkin out ya bikini bod!!

Me: I bet it won't.

Bea: I've Googled Stråla. Amazeballs. It's beautiful!

They have these cows with the biggest brown eyes EVER!

Pearl: **Shut up and get a tan. At least you're not stuck in this dump.**

I've told them I'm going to ring every single day so I don't get lonely. The boat tips gently from side to side. I turn over my warm pillow and check my phone. No new messages. There's a knock at the door and Frida peeks in. 'Still awake, Katrina?'

Only my Swedish relatives ever call me this. 'It's so hot,' I say, flopping my arms above my head.

'There will be a lovely breeze on Stråla.' Mushrooms, cows, sheep . . . and a breeze! Frida squeezes past my bulging suitcase and sits on the end of my bed, arms wrapped round her knees. She's wearing a chunky fisherman's jumper and her face is a strange green colour from the lights on the quay. 'I just came to say goodnight,' she says, 'and to say sorry you are feeling so sad.'

'It's not your fault.' I want to tell her that I'm dreading it, that I can't imagine what I'll do every day, that already I feel homesick, actually really and truly sick in my stomach . . . But if I do that, I'll start to cry. I pull the pillow closer and we listen to a couple outside arguing in Swedish. I can't make it all out, but it's something to do with him 'stroking Astrid'.

'Hey,' says Frida, patting my legs. 'It's not what you were expecting, but sometimes that's when the best things take place. Magic happens on Stråla.'

'I don't believe in magic,' I mutter.

'That's because you've never been to Stråla!' Her eyes glitter. 'And Leo might be there. You'll like him.'

Leo. One word, that's all it takes. I sit up. 'Who's Leo?'

'He's a boy I met last time I was there, a bit older than you, I think. His family stay on Stråla.'

'What's he like?' I ask, unable to hide the pathetic glimmer of hope I'm feeling.

'You know, he's . . .' Frida hesitates as she tries to find the right word, '*ypperlig*.'

Ypperlig. One of those funny words that don't really

36

have an English equivalent. Mum always says it about Dad. It means 'perfect', in just the right way. The woman's deluded.

Ypperlig Leo, on the other hand . . .

'Plus,' says Frida, kneeling up on my bed to peer out of the porthole, 'in a few days' time there will be a full moon, and then, gradually, it will disappear until it's completely hidden. Amazing!' She looks back at me. 'It's a time of new beginnings, Kat, growth and love. It's called a *dark* moon. Isn't that beautiful?'

She kneels up a bit higher, trying to get a better view from the porthole. Peeking out below her chunky jumper is her pale pink bottom.

'Frida, I think I can see it . . . I can see the dark moon!'

'What? Where?' She sticks her head further out of the porthole.

'Attached to the top of your legs, not covered in a pair of *pants* like it should be.'

'Ha!' Frida laughs. 'It's too hot for underwear.'

'But you've got a jumper on.'

'I didn't want to embarrass you,' she says.

'Thanks.'

'No worries.' She gets up, has a good long embarrassing stretch, then goes to the door. '*Godnatt måne*,' she says. It's what Mum always says to me at bedtime.

'Goodnight moon,' I reply.

As soon as she's gone, the homesick feeling creeps back. I roll over in the hard bed and think about home. Usually, Britta's the last one to go to bed. After she's finished her college work, she watches TV until late to try and relax. I like hearing the muffled sound of the TV. Sometimes, if she's watching something funny, I hear her laughing. She's got a really weird, snorty laugh.

I actually miss *Britta*. I try not to think about her horrible dressing gown that she's been wearing since she was twelve, or the way she bites her nails like she's nibbling a nut, because for some strange reason this makes me feel even sadder. Instead, I think about meeting Ypperlig Leo. I imagine lying on a beach, sunbathing in my Roxy bikini, and a shadow falling over me. I peer over the top of my (new yellow) sunglasses and see a tall blond Scandi God.

'I'm Leo,' he says, gazing into my eyes. Clearly, he thinks I'm beautiful. It's love at first sight.

The boat sways and suddenly my fantasy Leo is wearing Britta's grey dressing gown. Annoying. I replace the dressing gown with board shorts and a ripped chest and I make him say, 'Do you need some help with that suntan lotion?' But then Leo starts to bite his nails and snorty-laugh, so I give up trying to control my mind and fall asleep.

FOUR

'Next stop, Stråla!' says Frida as the boat pulls away from the jetty. The horn blasts and thick grey smoke pours out of the funnel. We're sitting on the deck at the back of the boat, our feet resting on chairs, faces tilted to the sun. For the past two hours we've been cruising between islands, as the boat picks up and drops off holidaymakers. It looks like we're the only passengers left. I take this as a bad sign.

'Time for *fika*?' asks Frida. She's big on Swedish traditions, including having coffee and cake at eleven on the dot.

'Sure, but can I have Coke instead of coffee?'

She rolls her eyes. 'OK, but it's all wrong.' She sets

off across the deck, clinging to the backs of chairs to keep her balance. 'You're fifty per cent Swedish, Kat,' she calls back. 'You need to embrace your inner Swede!'

I lean back in my chair and shut my eyes. The vibrations from the engine are making me feel sleepy. Suddenly, I remember that I haven't done my nails and I rummage in my bag for my make-up. Frida rushed me this morning and when I got out of the shower, she was ready to go. I didn't even have a chance to straighten my hair.

By the time she comes back with our drinks, I've applied two messy coats of 'Alexa Cashmere'.

'Pretty colour,' she says.

I hold my hand out in front of me. My nails are a soft pinky-white. 'It goes with the sea,' I say.

'You're just like your mum. She's good with colours.' Mum paints watercolour pictures. I can only paint nails. I got a D for my last piece of art homework. As we sip our drinks, I get out my phone. 'You'd better use it quickly,' says Frida. 'You'll lose reception soon.'

'I've only got two bars. I'll wait until we get to the island.'

'Nope.' Frida holds her cup in the air as we're rocked by a wave. 'Can't do that. There's no reception on the island.'

'What?' I stare at her. 'Are you sure? Hasn't every-where in the *world* got reception now?' My voice rises with panic. 'An eighty-year-old man climbed Everest and rang his daughter from the top. It's true. We saw it in geography. If Everest has reception, then Stråla must have it.'

Frida shakes her head. 'No reception. You're going to have a holiday from technology. Isn't that exciting?'

'Frida, once I left my phone in my locker at school and when I realised, I *cried*.' Frida laughs. I don't think she realises this isn't supposed to be a funny story. 'How will I talk to my friends?'

'You can write to them. The postal service is excel-lent. Letters get to the UK in three days, and they can send letters to you.'

I look down at my phone. One bar left. Do my friends even know how to write a letter?

'Quick, Frida,' I say. 'I need the address.' As I write my text, the single bar on my phone keeps vanishing and reappearing. **No phone reception on Stråla. DISASTER. Please, please, please send me a letter TODAY.** I add the address and then sign off: **Don't forget me!! Kat xxxxxx**

I send the message to Bea, Betty and Pearl, although there's almost zero chance Pearl will write to me. She doesn't even write in school. The single bar disappears. I stare at the screen. One, two, three minutes pass. My phone is useless, just a great big watch. I sip my Coke and keep glancing down at it, forgetting that nothing will appear. To stop myself, I shove it in my bag.

'Oh, look, Kat!' Frida leaps to her feet and peers over the rail, her skirt blowing in the wind. 'I can see Stråla.'

I stand next to her and she points to a distant island. Until now, there have been so many islands in the

43

archipelago that it's almost been crowded, but Stråla looks like it's the last one. It's a lump of pine trees and grey rock. That is it. Beyond Stråla is the open sea, and beyond that . . . I don't know. Finland, I guess.

Mum and Dad have sent me to the end of the world.

'It's so wonderful to be back,' says Frida, as we pull the last pieces of our luggage off the jetty. An old man was waiting for us and now he starts to chuck our bags into a trailer attached to his scooter. He's wearing a blue cap pulled low on his head and a yellow tracksuit that is so seventies it's actually cool. His brown face is covered in deep wrinkles. My suitcase won't quite fit so he starts pounding it with his fist.

'Careful,' I say. 'My straighteners are in there.' He stops what he's doing and turns to stare at me. 'They're GHD . . . IV . . . the jade ones.' He blinks, slowly, and continues to stare like I'm speaking in a foreign language, which I suppose I am.

Frida is crouched on the floor picking some wild

flowers. She looks up. 'This is my niece, Kat,' she says in Swedish. 'She's English.'

The old man nods as if this explains everything. 'Otto,' he growls. Then he turns round and carries on pounding my case until it fits in the gap.

Once everything is loaded on to the trailer, Frida's guitar balanced on the top, we set off along the track. It was Frida's idea to bring the guitar. She says I can play to her in the evenings while she meditates. So depressing.

Otto drives at a snail's pace so that he can answer all of Frida's questions about Judit's chickens and Alvar's new shed. 'You know, Kat,' says Frida, switching to English, 'Otto's scooter is the only vehicle on the island.' We're walking along a sandy path through a forest. 'He's just been telling me about the plans for the festival tomorrow.'

'Festival?' My ears prick up, although I know we're not talking Glastonbury here.

'I forgot to tell you about it.' Frida links arms with me. 'Tomorrow there will be a little festival on the island, the Solsken Festival. Do you know what *solsken* means?'

Of course I know what *solsken* means – Mum's relatives love testing my language skills, but I never play along. 'Awesome famous rock bands?' I say.

'No, "sunshine", but there will be a band playing.'

'My band,' says Otto, speaking in heavily accented English.

'And a disco,' Frida adds.

'My disco,' Otto says. 'I run all the discos on Stråla.'

'Oh,' I say. He takes his eyes off the path and looks at me, like he's waiting for me to say something. 'You must like music,' I add.

He grunts, then says, 'Sometimes Leo helps me. He's arriving soon.' Then, with a roar, he accelerates ahead of us and disappears round the bend.

'Ypperlig Leo,' I say under my breath.

'What?' Frida asks, tucking a flower behind her ear.

'Oh, nothing. Just daydreaming.'

★

It doesn't take long to get to the cabin Frida's rented. Like most cabins in Sweden, it's small and square and painted red and white. Unlike most cabins in Sweden, it's falling apart. One of the windows is cracked and paint is peeling off the wood in long curling strips. A scruffy garden of dry grass leads to a pebbly beach.

Otto swings our bags on to the porch. *Crunch*, Frida's silver furnace lands on my case, followed by a huge bag of groceries and then the guitar. Frida and I rush to help with the rest of our stuff before anything is broken. 'OK,' Otto says, dropping a set of keys in Frida's hands. 'Enjoy.' Then he frowns and stares at the horizon for a moment before stomping back to his scooter and driving up the track.

The sound of the engine fades and we stand in silence. Frida breathes deeply. 'Perfect,' she says.

'Mm,' I say, which is as close as I can get to the truth without hurting her feelings.

'Come on. I'll show you round.' She unlocks the

door, but it's stuck in the frame. She kicks it until it swings open.

I peer into the gloomy room. 'Are you sure we'll both fit in there?'

'You're so funny,' she says. 'This was Otto's family's cabin. When he was a boy, six of them used to stay here every summer.' I follow her inside. The walls are made of rough wooden planks and the floor is cracked concrete with faded rag rugs thrown over it. There's a stove in one corner and a table covered in a checked cloth. The whole place looks like it should be in a museum. 'Let's get some air in here.' Frida pulls back the lace curtains and flings open the windows.

She points to two doors. 'My room and the shower room,' she says. 'You're upstairs.' I can't see any stairs. Then I spot a hole in the ceiling and a ladder leaning against the wall.

Taking care not to chip my nail varnish, I prop the ladder against the hatch and climb into the attic. I step into a tiny room and the roof slopes so dramatically that

I can only stand up in the middle. It's boiling up here. I push open the window. The floor and ceiling – there are no walls – were painted white a long time ago and there's another stripy rug on the floor. The bed is a double mattress. That's it. Except for a light, there is *nothing* else in the room. No mirror, no wardrobe, no plug sockets.

No plug sockets!

'Wahooo!' yells Frida. Through the window, I see a streak of pink flash down the beach and crash into the sea. Frida's first skinny dip of the holiday. She floats on her back, kicking in circles. '*Hej!*' she calls out, seeing me at the window.

'Frida, does the cabin have electricity?'

'No. Just a gas stove and paraffin lamps.' So when the batteries run out this means no phone, no iPad, no iPod and no *straighteners*. Without straighteners, I look like Britta!

'Fancy a swim?' Frida shouts.

I shake my head. My chest aches. The cabin is so dark, so small and dusty, and I've just discovered that I can't use any of the things I love. I haven't even got anything to read. The only entertainment I have with me that doesn't require electricity is one copy of *Grazia*. And make-up. How am I going to survive a whole month here? This room is suffocating me. I can't bear to be in here for another minute.

'I'm going to go for a walk,' I call out, possibly for the first time in my life.

'Take as long as you like,' Frida says, her eyes shut. 'There are no rules here.'

FIVE

I grab the brochure that Frida gave me and set off along the winding path. I need something to do. I need to *buy* something. I'll go to the shop. An ice cream will make me feel better.

At the top of the path, I stop and look at the map. It is so simple it could be a joke. There are two 'roads' on Stråla: one that goes around the edge of the island, and one that cuts across the middle. On the opposite side is the buzzing heart of the island: the Beach Deck Cafe, a shop, a youth hostel and a hotel. I decide to walk around the edge of the island, guessing that I'll end up by the cafe in a couple of hours. I haven't a clue what I'll do this afternoon. Probably read *Grazia* . . . or go to sleep.

Twenty minutes later, I'm standing outside the cafe. It's shut. I've explored half of the island in twenty minutes, leaving me twenty-eight and a half days to explore the other half.

On the way, I passed a few people carrying rolled-up towels, but that was it. Oh, and lots of trees. And some rocks. I didn't even see any cows. Still, the empty cafe looks surprisingly OK. It has a deck stretching over the sea, long benches topped with white cushions and a chalk board advertising *kaffedrinkar, pommes* and *alkoholfritt*. I don't know what *alkoholfritt* are, but I know Pearl would like them.

I quickly check out the harbour in case any of the boats look like they belong to billionaires (nope), then walk across a grassy area the map says is the *mötesplats*. A noticeboard advertises tomorrow's Solsken Fest, which kicks off at three with the Otto Orkester Dansband, with Disco Otto taking over at 9 p.m. Through the trees, I see a plastic polar bear licking an ice cream. The shop! Stuff to buy . . . lipgloss . . . magazines . . . who knows!

It's cool and dark inside. I drift up and down the aisles, wishing my friends were here with me. There are so many bizarre things they'd love: bubblegum and popcorn-flavour sweets, a banana lolly you can peel, packets of digestive biscuits that cost *four pounds* and, best of all, *tampongs*. *Tampongs* are tampons!

Quickly, I take a selfie of me holding a box of *tampongs*. I wish I could send it to my friends. We could start a band called the Tampongs. Obviously, Betty and Bea would have to stop hating Pearl, but it could happen. I want to tell them this right now. Then I remember I can't. Ahhhhh!

I stare at my useless crappy phone, then look up and see a shelf stacked with stationery. I pick up a pack of paper and envelopes decorated with hedgehogs. That's what I'll do this afternoon: I'll write letters to my friends and tell them that we're going to form a ground-breaking girl rock band called the Tampongs!

I get a Hello Kitty lolly out of the freezer and go to pay.

There's a small queue at the till. An old lady wearing dungarees is resting on the counter, talking about herring, and standing behind her are a boy and a girl who are arguing over whether to buy a bag of Flamin' Hot Cheez Cruncherz or a tube of RäkOst paste. I'm pretty lazy with my Swedish, but an argument is always worth translating.

'I'm a vegetarian, you *arsel*!' yells the girl, as she tries to prise the paste out of the boy's hands. From the tutting of the dungarees woman, I'm guessing *arsel* is not a nice word. She picks up her shopping basket and leaves the shop.

Next, the boy calls the girl a '*dumskalle*' – which definitely isn't a nice word – drops a note on the counter and walks out of the shop carrying the RäkOst.

The girl stares at the Cheez Cruncherz she's still holding.

'Are you going to buy those?' asks the lady behind the counter.

'I haven't got any money, Juni.' The girl looks at the crisps then turns to me, opens her eyes wide and says, 'Can you lend me ten kronor?' She blinks. Her eyes are lined with very badly applied purple eyeliner. 'I'll pay you back.'

'Erm . . . OK,' I say, handing her the coins.

'Hey, you're English!' she says, quickly switching languages. While she pays for her crisps, I check out her look. She's wearing pink high-tops, denim culottes and a T-shirt that says 'Awesome and Beefy'. I pay for my lolly and we leave the shop. 'So, hi, I'm Nanna,' she says as she rips open the crisp packet, 'and that moron squirting paste in his mouth is Sören. My twin. Can you believe we're twins?'

'Well, I –'

'I know. Shocking. We look *nothing* like each other.' They look exactly like each other: Sören is Nanna, but he's wearing less make-up. Even their curly blonde hair is cut the same way. 'Who are you?' Nanna asks.

'Me? I'm Kat.'

'*Weird* name,' says Nanna, which is so hypocritical it's not even worth taking up. 'Crisp? You wanna walk with me?'

'OK,' I say, because Nanna is the only teenager I've met on Stråla. Even so, I'm a bit worried about being seen with her.

Sören disappears into the trees. 'He's shy,' says Nanna. 'Seriously. He'll probably never speak to you.'

As we walk, I tell her that I'm spending the summer on the island. 'I've only been here a couple of hours,' I say, 'and I'm already *so* bored.'

'Really?' she says, pushing her little pink glasses up her nose.

'Well, there isn't much to do.'

'There's *loads* to do! I've been coming here most of my life. C'mon, let's jump rocks.' She leads me off the path and down to the sea, and before I know it, I'm rock-jumping. Nanna flies off ahead of me, leaping from one huge grey rock to another. I hang back because I'm *fifteen*, and clearly this will destroy my nails (finger and toe). But then Nanna starts talking to me and I have to catch up with her to hear what she's saying.

It turns out, jumping on big rocks is dangerous in flip-flops. And *really* tiring. Nanna must have stronger thighs than me. She jumps around like a monkey while I crawl after her. It doesn't take her long to tell me her entire life story. She's thirteen and staying on the island in a cabin at the youth hostel. She's 'mad chatty' and Sören's 'mad quiet'; oh, and she loves 'mad cool' fashion, black-and-white films, gerbils and cold milk, but not orange juice because it's too 'spicy'.

'I can't jump any more,' I say, pulling myself on to a huge rock and flopping back. Nanna sits next to me and stops talking for a few blissful moments.

She can't last long. 'You see that rock,' she says, pointing out to sea. I force myself to lift up my head. The rock is quite a long way out and it looks like the back of a whale. 'Sometimes I get phone reception on that rock.'

I sit up properly and shade my eyes against the sun. The rock doesn't look like a grey lump any more: it's shining golden in the afternoon sun. 'Nanna,' I say. 'I am *so* glad I met you today.'

'Really?' She grins and hugs her knees. 'Me too! And we can go to Solsken together. Can you do the Little Frog dance? I can teach you how to do it!'

'My mum's Swedish,' I say. 'I can do the Little Frog dance. How long does it take to swim out to that rock?'

'About ten minutes. There are no currents. It's totally safe.'

'Ten minutes . . .' I'm not a bad swimmer. Along with playing the guitar, it's one of the few things I can do better than Britta.

'This summer is going to be so cool,' says Nanna, wriggling a bit closer to me. 'I've met you and Leo is coming for Solsken.'

'Leo?' I say, as if it's the first time I've ever heard the name.

'Wait until you meet him. He's really kind and, you know, into stuff. Kayaking, swimming, camping. The summer is always better when he's around.' She starts to throw little stones into the sea. 'Plus, he's *skön*.'

'You mean, he's sweet?'

'Yeah. He's yummy.' She grins at me. 'You know, hot.'

Save the important information until last, Nanna!

That evening, over spaghetti and soya meatballs, Frida tells me about Solsken Fest. We're sitting opposite each other at the table with the checked tablecloth. For the third time this evening, the paraffin lamp has gone out, so the room is lit with candles. 'The island gets busy for a couple of days,' says Frida, her wavy hair making crazy shadows on the wall. 'Every bed is taken, and tents are pitched all over the place. It's an excuse for another Midsummer, really.'

Midsummer is a big deal in Sweden, almost as big as Christmas. On the longest day of the year, everyone heads to the countryside to dress up in floaty clothes, drink loads of vodka and dance around a maypole. In the evening, they drink even more vodka and keep dancing. When I was little, I loved it. Especially the Little Frog dance.

'Will there be flower garlands?' I slap a mosquito that's landed on my foot.

'Sure, some people will make them. You and Britta used to look so cute making yours together.' Frida takes a sip of wine and her eyes glitter over the edge of her glass.

Nice. I'll work a garland into my outfit. I'm willing to do hippy chic for the right occasion. 'Pickled herrings? Bonfires? Barbecue?' I ask.

'Probably,' she says. 'Last year it was just *magic*. The sun didn't set until eleven o'clock at night and the party went on till morning. So romantic . . .'

But I've stopped listening. Instead, I'm visualising everything in my suitcase, trying to decide what to wear. I need to lay some clothes out on my bed. 'I think I might have a shower and turn in,' I say, taking my plate over to the sink.

'Really? I was thinking you could play the guitar. Or how about a sauna?'

'This place has a sauna?'

'In the shed by the jetty. It's heated by a wood burner, so I'll need to get it going.'

'Maybe another night.' Will I be too hot in jeans? I could wear my skinny jeans with a really loose shirt. 'Frida, is there any hot water here?' I've got the tap turned on full to wash up, but the water is still icy.

'Sometimes.'

'But not tonight.'

'No. Hey, jump in the sea if you want a wash. That's what I'm going to do.'

I try to scrub at the greasy marks on my plate. Another mosquito buzzes around my ear. 'No thanks.'

I leave my kind-of clean plate on the draining board and go to the ladder. '*Godnatt måne*,' I say, but I don't think Frida hears me. She's collecting logs from a basket under the sink and singing a song about elves.

I've decided what I'm going to wear to Solsken. I look at the short flowery dress, thin white belt and cropped cotton jumper that I've laid over my bed and I know it looks good. The only problem, of course, is shoes. I've brought five pairs with me, but none of them look right. I decide to sort it out in the morning.

Before I turn out the light, I get out my hedgehog paper and write two letters: one for Betty and Bea, and one for Pearl.

Dear Beatty
   Sorry you have to share a letter, but I can't be bothered to write two. I am <u>so</u> sad. I'm on Strála and it's <u>TINY</u>. There is nothing here except rocks and trees. Seriously,

there isn't even any sand on the beaches. As far as I can tell, there are two teen-agers on the island and they are both freaks. Well, the girl is. I don't think I've laughed since I last saw you two. Tomorrow there is going to be a festival with a band and a disco and even though I know it's going to be the most tragic event in the world (even more tragic than Hattie's party when her dad flicked the light switch on and off to make strobe lights) I am actually excited about it.

One interesting thing has happened, or might happen. Everyone keeps talking about this boy called Leo who is turning up tomorrow. He's obviously some massive big deal on Strála. The word 'hot' has been used to describe him. I will be ready!

PLEASE PLEASE PLEASE write to me.

Love Kat xxxxxxxxxxxxxxxxxxxxxxxxxxxxxxxxx

P.S. Forgot to mention the most important thing: I might be able to text or ring you if I can swim out to a rock. There is the small possibility that I will drown doing it, but it's a risk I'm willing to take.

Hey Pearl

This is a letter ... bet you never thought I'd write you one of these!?! Anyways, this island I'm staying on is <u>smaller than Bluewater</u> ... also, it has 299 fewer shops than Bluewater. Let me make this clear: it has ONE shop. But this one shop does sell loads of liquorice products (chocolate, chewing gum, cakes) and I remembered that you like Liquorice Allsorts, so I thought you might like to know that I have access to liquorice everything.

I hope your summer is significantly less

crappy than mine.

Love Kat

P.S. If you write back to me, I will bring you back some liquorice babies. That is a promise.

I turn on my phone for a nanosecond to get their addresses, then put the letters by the attic hatch. I'll post them in the morning.

After I've turned off the light, I open my window as wide as it will go and lean out, trying to find some cool air. The sea is inky blue and so still it could be a painting. Small waves must be breaking somewhere because I can hear them. Next to the jetty is a shed. Smoke twists from its chimney and the window glows orange. I can see Frida's pink shape moving around inside.

I look up at the sky and try to imagine Bea, Betty and Pearl back at home, in our town, and what they will have done today. Maybe Bea and Betty met up and got milkshakes. Pearl would have got up late and spent ages online. She has all these different names she uses. Some I know about – like Peargirl and Peawitch – but she has loads of others she keeps secret. Sometimes, she spends entire lessons telling lies to random people online.

I can't believe yesterday morning I was at home. Right now, I feel like I'm on another planet. The moon is low in the sky, round and yellow, like it's cut out of paper. I lie back on my mattress, the wrong way round, so I can stare through the window at the stars.

Bea, Betty and Pearl can see those stars, so can my mum and dad all the way round the world in America. This doesn't make me feel better. My heart races. I feel tiny, like I've disappeared. I force myself to think about all the pairs of shoes I've left at home. Blue Converse . . . ballet flats . . . silver flats . . . spotty wellies . . . Nikes . . . suede ankle boots (brown) . . . suede ankle boots (black) . . . I work through every pair I own and then I start again at the beginning.

My eyes start to close. Shoes work so much better than sheep.

SIX

As I walk back from the shop, I pass a line of passengers who've just got off the boat. Some are carrying rucksacks and others are pulling trolleys loaded with bags and tents. Children run in and out of people's legs, screaming at each other, and I have to step off the track to let a group of singing men go past.

I find Frida sitting cross-legged on the jetty, making us flower garlands. 'One for you,' she says, putting it on my head. 'So cute!'

I take it off to check she's not put anything mad in it, but it's just a band of daisies, ivy and a couple of blue ribbons. 'Thanks,' I say. 'Cinnamon bun?' I pass her the bag. I couldn't resist getting some when I went to post my letters. After ABBA, cinnamon buns are Sweden's best invention. 'The island's getting busy. I saw Otto building a stage on the *mötesplats* with some other ancient trolls.'

'He may be ancient, but he's probably fitter than you. All summer he rents kayaks and most days he swims to Fejan' – she points to the island in the distance – 'and then comes back on one of his kayaks. The next day he does the journey the other way round, paddling out and swimming back.'

'What's the other island called?' There are two little islands just off the coast of Stråla.

'Vilda. It means "wild". It's very beautiful. We'll have to go out there one day.'

'Sounds tiring.' I stretch my legs out in front of me and wriggle my toes. I've painted them a lush colour: minty green.

'*Hej!*' bellows a voice from somewhere in the woods. We turn round and watch as a bearded man leaps out from the pines. 'Frida, it's me!' he cries in Swedish. 'I came back!'

Frida jumps to her feet, dropping her garland and scattering flowers all over the deck. 'Nils!' she says, putting out her arms. He runs to her and wraps her up in a huge hug. Nils has wild blond hair and an even wilder beard. He's wearing an open shirt and tattoos cover his arms. Also, he has on way too many beads: round his neck, his wrists, his ankles, even in his beard.

They stare into each other's eyes, lost for words. 'I can't believe you're here,' whispers Frida, lifting a bead out of the way so she can give him a kiss.

Well. This is awkward.

I stand up and the creaking jetty makes them turn round.

'Oh, Nils,' says Frida, stepping back, 'this is my niece from England, Kat.'

'*Hej*,' says Nils, blushing. He reaches forward and shakes my hand. 'Welcome.' Like Otto, he has a strong accent. 'Very pretty flowers,' he says seriously, nodding at my garland.

Why didn't Frida tell me about Nils? Is he her

boyfriend? She must have been gutted when Mum asked if I could stay with her this summer. She'd probably been imagining a summer of saunas and skinny dipping with Beardy-beady Nils, but here I am, ruining it all. 'I might go and see if there's water for a shower,' I say.

'Stay and chat,' Frida says. 'Nils is a friend I met last year. I didn't know he was coming back . . . Well, I hoped he was.' Once again, I'm forgotten as they lock eyes.

'I think I'll get ready for the festival.'

But they haven't heard me. 'Cinnamon bun?' Frida asks as they walk hand in hand to the end of the jetty.

Standing under the 'shower' – a trickle of cold water dribbling from a rusty shower head – I realise two things: I'm not going to see much of Frida this summer, and I am *never* going to rinse my hair.

'Are you sure I look alright?' I ask Frida, again.

'Yes!' she says, but she doesn't even glance at me. 'Come on.' She pulls me along the track towards the music and laughter. 'No one cares what you look like at Solsken.'

That's exactly why I keep asking if I look OK. I don't want to be the only person who's made an effort. I want to look *just right*, then I can relax and maybe enjoy myself. There are no mirrors in the cabin and I had to do my make-up using the mirror on my blusher. Worst of all, I couldn't use my hairdryer or straighteners. Frida's told me that my hair looks 'really funky', which is worrying. Frida got ready for the festival in eight seconds: five to take off her shorts and vest and pull on a dress, and three to put her flower garland on.

She looks just right. *Ypperlig*.

The *mötesplats* is transformed. Bunting flutters between trees and Swedish flags are flying everywhere: in hair, cakes, ice creams and on the stage. Otto's band is in full swing. He's playing the accordion and his expression is serious, like he's performing at a funeral. Right now, his band are rocking out with 'It's Raining

Men'. The area in front of the stage is packed with dancers.

A welly shoots past my head. '*Okej!*' yells the man who's thrown it, jumping into his friend's arms and giving him a big hug.

'Welly throwing,' says Frida.

'Kat!' Nanna runs up to me and grins, bouncing up and down on her feet. At least one person wants me around. 'Wow. You look so . . . funky,' she says, admiring my skater dress and wavy hair. Funky. I want to go back to the cabin, curl up on the deck and read *Grazia* (again).

'I really like your –' I scan her outfit, trying to find something to compliment – 'T-shirt. It's funny.' She's wearing her high-tops again, but this time with a neon skirt and T-shirt. The T-shirt has a cartoon troll on it wearing a tracksuit. The troll appears to have an explosion coming from its bottom and he's saying, 'I just did a *fartlek*!'

'*Very* funny,' she says. 'Because *fartlek* is when you train fast then slow, and *fart* is when –'

'I get it,' I say.

'Come on.' She puts her arm through mine. 'Let's enter the three-legged race.'

I'm about to say that I should probably stay with Frida, but I realise Frida has disappeared. I spot her by the beer tent doing some intense gazing with Beardy-beady. 'I'll watch,' I tell Nanna, slipping my arm out of hers, but she just grabs hold of me again and drags me across the *mötesplats*.

Over the next few hours, I follow Nanna round the festival and watch her throw horseshoes, bob for apples, eat pickled herring and take part in a pass-the-potato race using spoons in mouths. Virtually everyone except me competes in the potato race. As I watch the potato move from person to person, and listen to the crowd roar with laughter as a huge man passes the potato to a toddler, I get this ache inside me. Even though I'm in a crowd of people, I feel on the edge and alone. Plus, Leo hasn't come. I'd have noticed if a *skön* boy turned up.

As the sun begins to set, the band stop playing and there's a pause in the festival as Otto starts the disco. Nanna and I sit on a rock by the cafe, sharing some chocolate kringles. The sun is still warm on my face. I throw a bit of my biscuit to a seagull who's been watching me with his tiny yellow eyes. 'You should have joined in with the Little Frog dance.' says Nanna. 'It's stupid, but it makes you happy.'

'I enjoyed watching.' Nanna is sweet, but hanging out with her is nothing like hanging out with my friends. With Bea and Betty, I laugh all the time, and Pearl is very funny, even if the things she says are some-times so mean that I feel bad laughing. I look out to sea, right at the horizon, and wonder if, right now, a plane is bringing a letter to me from one of them.

'I guess Leo couldn't make it,' she says, out of nowhere. 'Hey! Look at Otto. He's put on his disco waistcoat.'

Otto is standing behind his decks, fiddling with buttons and looking as cross as ever. He's changed the black waistcoat he was wearing earlier for one covered with smiley rave faces. He leans forward, turns on the microphone and taps it with his finger. A loud crackle of static bursts into the clearing.

'Every year,' says Nanna, 'after Solsken, Otto organises this really fun race, Tuff Troll, for all the young people staying on the nearby islands. It's an endurance race where you run across Stråla, swim to Fejan and then kayak back to Stråla. You have to be thirteen to take part, so Sören and I can enter this year.'

'I try to avoid race situations,' I say. There is nothing Britta likes more than a race. When we were younger, she'd make me have a toast-eating race with her when we got in from school. Britta can pack away a lot of toast. 'When is Tuff Troll?'

'On the twenty-fourth of August. It starts late in the afternoon and everyone gets back before the sun sets. Afterwards, there's a big party and the island is really busy because of all the people who've come for the race.'

'We're leaving the day after. I can watch you being a tuff troll.'

'Cool!'

Otto taps the microphone again. 'Testing, testing,' he says, then he waits for everyone to give him their full attention. Gradually, the chatter dies down. In Swedish, he delivers a lecture about litter then, after a dramatic pause, asks, '*Är du redo att rocka?*' Slowly, a crowd gathers in front of him. 'I said . . .' he sounds genuinely annoyed, '*Are you ready to rock?*' This time he gets some whoops and cheers. He watches the crowd, eyes narrowed, until he's satisfied with the level of enthusiasm. 'OK. Let's get down to . . .' he pauses to pull on a huge pair of headphones, '. . . Sexy Disco!'

He says 'Sexy Disco' in English. It's pretty funny. What he actually says is, 'Seckseee deescow!' Electronic music booms across the *mötesplats*. I was expecting total disco cheese, but this is serious dance music. Almost immediately, people of all ages take to the dance floor and start waving their arms about. Otto

77

growls, 'Oooo yeahhhh!' into the mike and starts busting shapes with his hands.

'Come on,' says Nanna, trying to pull me up.

'I'm not really in a dancing mood,' I say, knowing how annoying I sound. Nanna shrugs and goes off to join everyone else. Soon Otto abandons his Euro disco for big crowd-pleasers and I watch as Nanna jumps around to 'Super Trouper' and 'Guantanamera'. She's dancing all on her own, but she doesn't care.

Just as I'm wondering if Frida would mind if I went back to the cottage, something magical happens.

There's this pause as one track comes to an end and all the dancers freeze on the spot as they wait for the next song. Then, in the trees, fairy lights are switched on and at exactly the same moment the sun dips below the horizon, making everything glow orange. 'Holding Out for a Hero' blasts out of the speakers and the dancers spring back into action. My mum loves this song and she does this painful duet of it with Dad, usually when my friends are round.

For the tenth time that evening, Nanna turns to me and mouths, 'Dance!' And this time, I do. It turns out there is one other teenager in the world who knows all the words to 'Holding Out for a Hero' and she's wearing a *fartlek* T-shirt.

And that's how, somehow, I end up having fun.

SEVEN

While the disco's still raging, Frida and I head back to the cottage. We walk through the wood, the moon lighting up the path and pine needles crunching under our feet. Frida is so happy she almost dances home, and as soon as we get to the cottage, she runs down the path, across the beach and straight into the sea. She paddles around in the shallows. 'It's so beautiful,' she says, kicking up water. 'Look how low the moon is, Kat. It's almost touching the water!'

I slip off my shoes and walk into the sea. The water is perfect: cool and warm, all at the same time. I close my eyes and tilt my face to the sky. 'Look, Frida.' I stretch my arms above my head. 'I'm moon-bathing!'

'How about moon-swimming?' Without waiting for an answer, Frida pulls her dress over her head.

I look out to sea. It's temptingly still and I'm hot from dancing. 'Yeah, why not?' I say, surprising myself.

Frida is about to take off her bra when she notices me still standing there. 'I suppose you want a swimming costume?' she says. 'I'll grab mine off the washing line and you can change in the sauna.' Before I can say anything, she runs back up the beach and disappears round the side of the cottage.

Water laps around my legs and on the far side of the island, 'La Bamba' is thumping out. My toes feel blissfully cool. I wriggle them in the water and stare at the moon's reflection. It's such a hot night. I pull my dress away from my sticky body.

Suddenly, I have a mad urge to dive into the sea. I'm going to do it *right now* – I'm going skinny dipping! I take off my dress, scrunch it into a ball and throw it on to the beach. Then, hardly believing what I'm doing, I pull off my underwear and send it flying on to the pebbles next to my dress. I stand in the shallow water, totally pantless, moon-bathing.

'Wow, look at my crazy niece.' Frida reappears holding her costume and a couple of towels. 'The moon's made you go mad.'

I do feel a bit crazy, like I want to make up for wasting most of the festival sulking and feeling sorry for myself. 'Watch this, Frida,' I say. 'I'm going to do the Little Frog dance!' Then I start singing, '*Små grodorna, små grodorna!*' at the top of my voice, and I do the dance, jumping up and down in the water and wiggling my hands on my bottom to make a tail. Nanna's right: the Little Frog dance does make you happy!

Frida joins in on the shore and bounces towards me. '*Kou ack ack ack, kou ack ack ack!*' we sing, while we squat up and down doing frog jumps.

'*Kou ack ack ack!*' I go . . . Then I notice Frida has stopped singing and is staring out to sea. 'What is it?' I say. But she ignores me, raises her hand and waves. She's waving at someone *behind me*!

'*Hej*, Leo!' she calls out.

'*Hej*.' A deep voice, clear and distinct, drifts towards us.

Oh my God. *Leo is somewhere on the sea!* With lightning speed, my mind runs through the options: run for the cottage and he'll see my naked jiggling bottom; turn round and he'll see my naked jiggling boobies and *front* bottom! I do the only thing I can do: throw myself face down in the sea. I enter the water so hard my body slams into the pebbles. Too late, I realise the shallow water barely covers me.

'Are you OK, Kat?' asks Frida. I'm on all fours coughing up sea water.

'Yeah . . . Just swimming.' I crawl away from the shore, desperately hoping the water will get deeper. It's slow going. I keep crawling until water laps over my bum. Only then do I dare look up. A few metres in front of me is a canoe. A boy is watching me, his paddle resting across his lap.

'*Hej*,' I say, moving forward. 'I'm Kat.' And I actually stick my hand out of the water like we're at a business meeting or something.

Leo reaches over the side of the canoe and shakes my hand. '*Hej*,' he says, politely keeping his eyes fixed on my face. 'I'm Leo.'

Is he smiling? It's hard to tell. Frida wades out towards us. Somehow, she's managed to put on her costume. This is so unfair! 'Leo,' she says, 'you've missed the festival.'

'I tried to get here in time.' As he speaks, I crawl deeper into the sea so that I can crouch down, my arms folded tightly across my chest, water up to my chin. 'I've kayaked from Stockholm, wild camping on islands on my way here.'

'Wonderful!' says Frida, her face filled with admiration for his adventure, and then she starts to question him, *in detail*, about his trip while I keep myself wrapped up in a small ball.

'Some islands were deserted,' he says. 'I caught fish,

cooked them over fires.' Although I try not to stare, it's hard not to look at this person I've heard so much about. Even in the moonlight I can tell he's tanned and his hair is tangled with sea water, but he's no Scandi God. In fact, I can't believe how *ordinary* he looks. Except his arms. He's got impressive arms, which isn't really surprising because he's just canoed over fifty miles to get here.

'How long did it take?' asks Frida, dropping into the sea and elegantly floating on her back.

'About a week.' He glances down at me and I nod as though I'm considering this very seriously.

Then, out of nowhere, Frida says, 'Leo, it would be great if you could take Kat out on the sea.' There's a moment's silence. I can hardly bear to look at him. In the moonlight, his face is half hidden in shadows and hard to read, but I'm sure I see a frown flash across his face. 'She'd love to go, wouldn't you, Kat?'

'Well,' I say. 'I guess Leo is tired so –'

'I'm fine,' says Leo. 'I can take you.'

'Great!' says Frida. 'Tomorrow morning?' Oh, God. This is beyond embarrassing. I bet she wants the cottage to herself so she can be reunited with Beardy-beady.

'Um, OK,' he says.

What else can he say? If there were enough water, I'd bury my head in it. 'Honestly, you don't have to –'

'Tomorrow is the best time to go,' he says, interrupting me. 'I'm going to try to catch the end of the festival.' He starts to paddle away, his canoe moving swiftly across the bay. 'Bye, Frida,' he calls over his shoulder. 'See you tomorrow, Kat.'

We watch as his canoe cuts across the path of golden moonlight. 'So,' says Frida, rolling on to her front and smiling, 'you've met Leo.'

After I've dried off, removed my make-up and brushed my teeth, I realise I'm still blushing. I sit on my bed in my sauna (aka the attic) and find my hedgehog paper. What was worse: Leo seeing my special Frog Dance, or Frida forcing him to take me out for the day? I desperately want to text my friends: their jokes would make me feel so much better. I decide to get rid of the shame of what's just happened by writing a letter, but just to Betty and Bea: Pearl doesn't keep secrets.

Dear Beatty

So, I have met the famous Leo, Lord of Strála, God of the Scandi men, and I thought you would like to hear the news . . .

DISAPPOINTING!

Leo is:

★ Small (actually I have only seen him sitting in a canoe and he could have had long legs tucked away in there, but he appeared small)

★ Boring - he is totes into bees, flowers, tides and birds

★ Brown haired (again, not 100% on this as the moon was my only light source, but

defo got a brown vibe off him - no offence, Bea)
* In possession of an average face (I couldn't see much of it because of the night, but if it had been cutesome, surely I'd have noticed??)
* 6.5 out of 10
Positives:
* Ripped arms
That is all I can tell you, but I'm sure to bump into him soon as we are all essentially living together on Stråla. It's like *Big Brother*. My evil Auntie Frida made him agree to take me CANOEING tomorrow, but I'm not going because when she suggested it, he looked like he'd rather sniff one of Pinky's poos (when she's been eating salmon Sheba). Do you remember when Pinky did a poo on my blazer? Remember the smell? Freeze your face. That is what Leo looked

like when Frida asked him to take me canoeing.

Tomorrow, I'm going to get up early and hide somewhere on Stråla for the day to avoid canoeing humiliation.

OK. There is one other piece of news. I was butt naked when I met Leo. It's hard to explain how this came about, but trust me, it happened. Except for Mum, Dad, Britta and Frida, I think he may be the only person in the world who has ever seen me naked.*

I so badly need one of you here with me so I can pretend I don't care about the naked thing.

REALLY wish you were here.

xxxxKat.

*Bea, that time you walked in on me in the Topshop changing room doesn't count because I was wearing a bra. Betty, just to explain, my pants came off with the fake leather trousers I was trying on. They were <u>obscenely</u> tight.

I put the letter in the envelope, seal it and write on Bea's address. Then I leave it on the kitchen table.

I lie in bed trying not to think about Leo watching me do naked squats.

All I can think about is Leo watching me do naked squats.

Still blushing, I drift off to sleep.

Naked squats. Naked squats.

Naked.

Squats.

EIGHT

The next morning I creep out of the cottage with everything I need to occupy me on the beach for a few hours (bottle of water, towel and my wrinkled copy of *Grazia*), but as I'm shutting the cabin door, I hear a tell-tale splashing noise. With a sinking heart, I turn round. Leo is paddling across our bay, but this time he's in a canoe with two seats.

'Ready?' he calls out.

'Seriously?' I say. I can't help sounding annoyed. 'It's not even *eight*.'

'It's a long paddle and the sun's going to be hot.'

'I guess.' I try to think on my feet. I can't get out of this now, but I am so *not* ready: I'm wearing flip-flops, my trackie bum-bums over my bikini and my make-up is minimal. It's what I'd do for Sunday lunch at Grandma's. I'm Grandma-ready, not boy-ready!

Leo guides the canoe to the edge of our jetty and I go over to meet him. Daylight reveals that his hair is indeed brown and so are his eyes. I decide my six and a half was accurate and congratulate myself on my ability to rate boys in the dark. 'You've got a new canoe,' I say, because he's fiddling around with ropes and ignoring me.

'Kayak,' he says, climbing out and throwing a life jacket towards me. 'It's a tandem kayak.' OK. He isn't that short. I got that wrong. He starts to rearrange some bags he's got strapped to the back of the kayak, then, finally, he glances up at me and frowns. 'You need something that covers your shoulders,' he says. 'The sun can really burn on the sea.'

I spin round and go back into the cabin and up to my room. It's obvious that Leo doesn't want to take me out: he can barely look at me. Why did he even bother turning up? I pull on a shirt, then I curl my eyelashes and put on mascara. I glance out of the window. Leo is standing, arms folded, at the end of the jetty, staring out to sea. A bit of lipgloss and some perfume make me almost boy-ready. Leo might not want to take me kayaking, but I still want him to know he's snubbing a total fox.

When I get back to the jetty, he gives me a crash course in paddling. Then he tightens my life jacket (we have to stand weirdly close to do this), puts my bag in a watertight sack and holds the kayak steady while I climb in. He manages to do all this without making eye contact once.

He gets in behind me, pushes us away from the jetty, and we're off! In circles . . . Then we hit the jetty . . . Then we do two more circles and I drop my paddle and scream . . . Then we hit the jetty again. 'Sit still,' says Leo. 'If you hold your paddle across your lap, I'll get us clear of the bay.'

'Sorry,' I say, blushing. I hate Frida. I totally hate her.

'OK,' he says, once we're on the open sea. 'You can start paddling. We're heading for Vilda.'

At first, my paddle keeps shooting out of the sea, showering us with water, or I miss the sea entirely and the kayak rocks crazily from side to side. While I make a series of sounds (ow . . . woah . . . ah . . . urgh), Leo paddles us steadily forward.

It takes us a long time to go a very short distance, and sometimes we go backwards, but finally I get the hang of it and Vilda seems to be getting bigger. I know I'm doing OK because Leo, who has been this lurking silent presence behind me, suddenly says 'Good,' and I'm *really* pleased. How annoying.

As we wobble our way towards the island, I start to feel self-conscious about Leo staring at my back. It's a bit too close to what happened last night and, without being able to see his face, I can't tell what he's thinking. Maybe he's loving being out on the water with me, bathed in the golden rays of the morning sun, but I just can't shake the feeling that he'd rather not have

Frog-Dance-bum-girl dumped on him for the day. Eventually, I have to break the silence. 'Frida told me that you've been staying on Stråla for years,' I say.

'Yes,' he says, clearly and politely.

'Are you in a cabin?'

'No.'

'The youth hostel?'

'No.'

'Hotel?'

'A tent.' Silence (except for the splash of our paddles). Then Leo says, 'It's a nice tent.'

'Oh my God, I hate camping,' I say. 'My dad takes me and my sister – Mum won't go because of the toilets – and I have to sit around in a field feeling cold and playing Candy Crush on my phone. Dad tries to get us all to play cricket, but, *as if?* There are only three of us.' Silence. 'So, what do you like doing when you're not canoeing –'

'Kayaking.'

'. . . when you're not *kayaking?*'

'I like running, sailing, nature, football . . . and the sea. I love the sea.' He pauses, then says, 'What are your hobbies?'

'I like doing loads of stuff,' I say, then I realise shopping for the ultimate pair of boots, making your friends laugh by imitating your teachers, and watching kitten films on YouTube probably don't count as 'hobbies'. 'I play the guitar,' I say, 'and I dance, but generally I hate sport and I can take or leave nature . . . Stars are nice.' Our paddles splash through the sea. 'Clearly, we've got loads in common, Leo.'

After a moment, he laughs. 'That's funny,' he says. 'Sorry, sometimes I'm slow at translating. I like listening to the guitar, and you think stars are OK, so maybe we aren't that different.' This makes me smile. However, despite the discovery of these two amazing shared interests, we still paddle in silence the rest of the way to Vilda.

'What do we do now?' I ask. We're standing on a small

beach, the kayak pulled high out of the water. In front of us is nothing but sea. We can't even see Stråla. Just in case there's reception, I turn on my phone. Nothing, not even one pathetic little bar. I drop it in my bag.

Leo shrugs. 'Explore?' Neither of us move. It reminds me of when Mum and Dad would visit friends and dump me and Britta in the garden with some strange children and tell us to go and play. Awks.

'What about our stuff?' I ask. Maybe we could just paddle back to the cabin. We'll have been away for nearly an hour.

'We're on an island in the middle of nowhere. Essentially, this is our island for the day.'

'*Our* island,' I repeat. This feels a tiny bit exciting.

'Come on. I'll show you around.' And Leo is off, scrambling over some rocks and up a bank. He looks back at me standing on the beach. 'We're going up there.' He points to the highest bit of the island. It's a hill. Not a mountain, just a hill, but still . . . With a groan, I dump my bag in the kayak and follow him. 'Watch out for adders!' he shouts as he disappears into the trees.

I'm limping by the time I get to the top. Leo's standing on a ledge of rock taking in the view. On my way up, I slipped and somehow got my foot stuck between two boulders. Leo had to pull me out, but one of my flip-flops wouldn't budge and we had to leave it behind. It's hard climbing with only one flip-flop. It was pretty hard climbing with two.

I stand next to him on the ledge and turn in a circle. I can see the entire island. It's like a miniature world with bays, pools, rocks and hills. Leo touches my arm. 'White-tailed eagle,' he says. I look at his hand resting on me.

'What?'

'Look.' He points at a cliff on our left. 'By that patch of thrift, just under the sea asters?'

'Double *what*?'

98

'By the white flowers, just under the yellow daisies.'

'Got it! Oh my God, it's massive! It's bigger than my cat . . . It could eat my cat!' We sit down on the rock and let our legs dangle over the edge.

'A female was spotted in Greenland that had a wing-span of two and a half metres.'

'Big?' I ask.

'Big,' says Leo, laughing. 'Look. It's about to fly.' Together we watch as the eagle launches off the cliff and swoops down over the sea.

'Whoa . . . those are huge wings.'

'The biggest you're ever likely to see.' The closer it gets to the water the more its muscly legs stick out. Its talons stretch wide like it wants to grab something.

'Uh-oh,' I say. 'I'm getting a bad feeling about this. Are we about to witness a murder?'

'Hopefully.' But the eagle's claws dip into the sea and come up empty. It skims over the surface of the water then rises. As it flies back over us, I can see every feather, a brown fluffy tummy and a hooked yellow beak.

'Do you like it?' asks Leo.

I nod and stare as it flies beyond the cliff. It might be the most amazing creature I have ever seen, and I own a bald cat. In front of me is the sea. Nothing but the sea. The sun is fierce and the water sparkles with a million flashing diamonds. 'Are we really the only people here?' I ask. Leo nods, and for a moment our eyes meet. He is almost smiling. I notice that his hair isn't really brown. In places it's bleached by the sun, almost as blond as mine.

'You don't need that flip-flop any more,' he says. We both look at my single flip-flop, which is dangling on my foot.

'I suppose I don't.' I take it off.

'Why don't you get rid of it?' Leo takes it out of my hands, leans back and throws it towards the sea. It windmills high over the rocks and lands on the branch of a pine tree.

I look at him, surprised. 'Hey, you just threw my flip-flop off a cliff!'

'Sorry.' He looks alarmed.

'I don't care,' I say, laughing, 'but isn't it against some Swedish nature law? A racoon might get its nose caught in it . . . or a white-tailed eagle.'

'It won't bother anyone up there.'

'What about an owl? An owl could get its wing tangled in the thong.'

'One day you can come back, and it will still be there.'

'With an owl skeleton attached to it.'

'The only owls we really get here are eagle owls. They're very big. Its wing couldn't fit in the thong.'

'A baby owl skeleton might be attached to it.'

'Seriously, it's fine,' he says, 'but if an island ecology ranger turns up – they won't, they don't exist – then I'll take the blame and go to prison. Come on,' he says, turning round. 'Let's eat. I'm hungry.'

Back at the kayak, Leo does something very surprising. He opens one of his waterproof bags, pulls out an embroidered tablecloth and sets up a picnic. I didn't even think about food today, but obviously Leo has. He opens Tupperware boxes and arranges two plastic plates and cups on the cloth.

'There,' he says, sitting back. 'I think that's everything.'

'What about flowers?'

'Flowers?'

'I'm joking. It looks great, really.' And it does. It looks so great I'm almost embarrassed.

'This is what Mum brings when we have a picnic.' He frowns and stares at the slices of cheese, ham and bread and the tub of boiled potatoes. He's even made sour cream and dill sauce and has brought a tiny tub of pickled juniper berries. Honestly? I'm not that keen on cold potatoes and rubbery Swedish cheese – I'm more of a McDonald's girl – but this is the cutest thing I've ever seen a hench boy do. 'Cranberry juice?' he asks.

Even cuter!

After we've had our picnic, which is lovely, but could

really do with a Twix or brownie to round it off, we lie back on the warm rock. 'Are you entering Tuff Troll?' I ask, staring at the sky.

'Yes. I've entered for the past few years, but never won it.'

'Maybe you will this year.'

'Maybe,' he says, then neither of us speaks. A bird circles over our heads. 'This year I'm entering with my friend Peter.' Again, we fall quiet. Leo studies the bird and I imagine what Peter looks like. Fingers crossed for a slightly taller, blonder, funnier version of Leo.

'OK,' Leo says, interrupting my naughty thoughts. 'We're going to swim to that headland.' He points across the bay to a bit of land that sticks out like a finger. 'Can you do that?'

'Yeah, probably,' I say. Oh my God. It's miles and I ate so many potatoes.

'Right. Let's go.' Leo stands up, pulls his T-shirt over his head, kicks off his Converse and strides towards the sea. 'Come on,' he says, over his shoulder. He stops at the water's edge when he realises that I'm still sitting on the rock, staring at him. 'What's the matter?'

I blink. 'Nothing. Just . . . not sure what stroke to do.' And checking out your muscles! *Wow. Congrats on the good shoulders, Leo. They've just pushed you to a seven.*

'Any stroke,' he says, then he nimbly jumps off the rock, wades out a few metres, dives into the sea, surfaces and breaks into a powerful front crawl, taking him to an impressive seven point five.

By contrast, I spend a few minutes taking off my clothes (behind a tree), crawl backwards down the rock on my hands and knees because it's covered in slippery weed, slip on the slippery weed, scream, shoot into the cold water and scream again (because I've trodden in something squidgy – hopefully slippery weed).

Leo has stopped swimming and is treading water, watching the show. I stand in the sea, splashing my arms and chest, saying, 'Oh . . . ow . . . oh . . . cold!' Leo's baffled face forces me into the freezing Baltic. I allow myself one final scream. Then, taking care to keep my nicely made-up face out of the water, I breast-stroke towards him. Leo switches to breaststroke too and we swim side by side towards the rock.

'I thought you hated sport,' Leo says.

'I do. PE is my worst lesson at school.'

'You've got a good stroke.'

'Oh, I used to do loads of swimming.' I think back to all the Saturdays I spent at the swimming club at our local pool, and the badges I made Mum sew all over my bag.

'So, let's race,' he says, then he starts doing front crawl and shoots ahead of me. No fair: he had a head start! Before I know what I'm doing, my face is down in the water and I'm swimming as fast as I possibly can. I keep my head steady and let my hips roll, just like my coach taught me. Soon my fingertips are level with Leo's feet. My chest feels like it might burst, but I get my breathing under control and push myself on, faster and faster.

But I can't catch him, and soon he moves ahead of me. I don't give up. It's been a long time since I swam fast, felt my body slip through the water and my heart race. As adrenalin floods my body, I remember how I loved Saturday mornings, the smell of chlorine and the pool, empty and still. I reach the bottom of the cliff a few seconds after Leo and cling on to a rock, gasping for breath, the sky spinning.

'Right,' says Leo, his voice perfectly steady. 'Now we climb.'

I look up. It's a small cliff, but essentially, it's a cliff. 'No way,' I pant. 'Too high.'

Leo shrugs. 'I just wanted to show you something. It doesn't matter.'

After a bit more panting, I say, 'What do you want to show me? I bet it's a view or a fern or something.'

'It's a Starbucks,' he says, straight-faced.

I stare at him for a moment then I look up. There are a lot of footholds and it isn't that high. 'Alright. I'll do it. But only because you made a joke.'

'You go first. I'll spot you.'

'Spot me?'

'I watch you from below and tell you where the grips are. If you fall, I'll make sure you do it safely.'

No way am I climbing a cliff in this bikini with Leo 'spotting me'. I bought it a size too small because it was the only one left in the sale. Let's just say the bottoms have a tendency to wedge. 'You go first,' I say. 'If I fall, I'll land in the sea. I'll get wet but I'll be fine.'

'But I can help you climb.'

'*You* go first.'

And, of course, Leo is up the cliff in seconds, like a mountain goat. I take it slowly, like a lazy, fifteen-year-old girl called Kat who has already pushed her body to the edge once today. Leo leans over the top giving me encouragement. 'Can you move your hand a few centimetres to the left? Well done! How about stretching yourself for this rock?'

'How about you shut up?' I yell. Sweat is pouring off me and my arm muscles are burning, but somehow I manage to haul myself up and over the final few feet of rock. I flop face down on dry scratchy grass, acutely aware of a wedge sensation but feeling too weak to do much about it. Never mind. He's seen it all before. 'Where's Starbucks?' I mutter. 'I need a Caramel Frappuccino.'

'No Starbucks,' he says. I force my head up. 'Just this.' He is standing on the other side of the platform staring over the edge.

Arms and legs wobbling, I get to my feet and join him. Together we peer down a wall of rock into a circular pool. The water is turquoise and sparkling.

'That looks so tempting,' I say. The sun is burning my shoulders and I'm sweaty from climbing. 'I'd like to just jump in.'

'Like this?' he asks. Then, with a huge leap, he launches himself off the cliff, flies through the air and lands in the centre of the pool. He disappears, then shoots to the surface with a massive 'Whoop!'

'Great,' I call down to him, legs still shaking from the climb. 'Now I'm stuck up here on my own!'

'You have to jump,' he says, pushing his hair back, '. . . or climb back down the way you came, but I wouldn't do that. It's dangerous.'

'It's too high for me. Seriously, Leo, I'm scared.' And I am. And annoyed. I can't tell if my pounding heart is from fear, the swim or anger that he's abandoned me up here.

'Don't be scared.'

'There might be rocks. Dad's always telling me never to jump into water unless I know how deep it is.'

'It's safe. I know these waters really well, but I'll check again.' Leo dives down. I can see him swimming a circuit of the pool. 'Definitely safe,' he says, when he comes up. 'You have nothing to be scared of.'

I stand on the edge of the rock, my toes dangling above the drop. I feel sick, and miles and miles away from Mum and Dad. 'Jump into the middle,' Leo shouts. I take a step back. He's at the side, looking up at me and treading water. He smiles. He should smile more often. It's a good smile. Definitely worth another half point.

I remember when I used to be fearless, when we spent our summer holidays by lakes in Sweden, and Britta and I would be in the water every day, diving, doing handstands and perfecting our synchronised swimming shows. 'Trust me.' This time Leo doesn't shout, but his voice still reaches me. He watches me with his dark eyes. I take a deep breath, then another, and then I shut my eyes and I jump. I fall through the sky, my arms and legs windmilling, my mind spinning, and I hit the water hard and plunge into deep, deep, cold water.

I kick towards the light and then Leo grabs my shoulders and he pulls me to the surface, and I'm gasping for air and laughing. We face each other in the pool. The only people on the island. I realise we're holding hands. 'I did it,' I say, amazed.

We tread water and Leo squeezes my fingers. Suddenly, I'm aware of everything: the drops of water hanging on Leo's hair, the ripples in the water, my thudding heart. 'I knew you would,' he says.

And that's when Leo jumps eight and hits nine.

★

Hours later, we head back to Stråla, taking even longer than we did this morning. It's getting late. Stråla's rocks glow orange in the evening light and the only sound is the splashing of our paddles. My hair is salty, my nails are chipped and I'm covered in sand and suntan lotion. Every muscle in my body aches. I feel amazing.

After I dive-bombed into the pool, Leo and I spent the rest of the day exploring the island. We swam in caves, jumped off rocks and climbed trees. I put my tracksuit bottoms on for that. They were prickly trees.

We ate everything Leo brought with him – dill-flavoured crisps, water warm from the sun and way too many Kex bars. As I was packing my stuff into the kayak, Leo disappeared for a few minutes. When he got back, he was carrying my flip-flop. 'The one in the rock is definitely stuck, but I managed to get this out of the tree,' he said. 'I kept thinking about that baby owl.'

As we paddle, I talk about home. I tell him about how my family are all fitness freaks. 'You'd like them,' I say. 'They're into races. When I was little, I was always having to race my sister – to the end of the road, up to bed, to the swings – and I always, always lost. I spent years chasing after Britta's bouncy ponytail. One day, I thought, what's the point? And I just stopped running.'

We pass the rock where Nanna said you can get phone reception. It is a long way from the beach, but after today, I think I can do it, and I have so much to tell my friends. 'What's that?' I ask Leo, pointing at a bird that has just popped out of the sea. So far, he's named every bird, flower and bit of moss I've pointed at.

'Sorry?' he says. He was a million miles away. 'Goldeneye, maybe.' That's it. Nothing about where it migrates to, what type of fish it prefers, why it's got such bulgy eyes. Maybe he's tired. It seems like the closer we get to Stråla, the quieter he gets. We paddle the last ten minutes in silence.

Back at the cabin, he holds the kayak against the jetty while I climb out. Smoke is drifting out of the sauna's chimney and I can hear Frida singing. 'Thank you for taking me to Vilda,' I say. Leo nods seriously and I stand there tapping my bare foot on the rotten wood. I have to say something else. 'It was fun,' I blurt out.

Shading his eyes against the sun, Leo looks up at me. I start to blush. 'I'd better go,' he says. 'Get this back to Otto.' He turns the kayak round.

'Oh, OK.'

When he's halfway across the bay, he stops and looks back. 'See you around?' he says.

I wave then walk towards the cabin. *It was fun*. It wasn't *fun*. Today I discovered a new kind of happy. I smile and hug my arms to my body. Frida sticks her head out of the sauna. 'Good day?' she asks. I nod. 'Do you want to come in?' Her cheeks are rosy pink, flushed from the heat.

'No thanks. I'm going to crash for a while.'

Back in the cabin, I take my letter to Bea and Betty off the table and tear it into strips, then I throw them in the recycling bin. Six point five . . . what was I thinking? Tomorrow I'm going to swim out to Reception Rock and tell Bea and Betty all about Leo. I can't wait.

NINE

I'm sitting on a beach Sellotaping my phone to my head. Like a seal . . . or a mermaid (cuter), I'm going to swim out to that rock, turn on my phone and get four massive bars of reception, followed by a tsunami of texts. Who knows, maybe I'll even check out some celebrity hairstyles and see if the Topshop sale has started! God, I love the internet.

I just wish that rock didn't look so dangerously far away.

It's taken me a while to perfect my Sellotape phone harness. I shake my head vigorously. Still too wobbly. I bite off another strip of tape and wrap it round my head. Nearly there.

This morning I hung out with Nanna. She taught me chess and I taught her airhead slang. Oh, and I may have mentioned Leo's name a few times. She said that spending the day with him must have been 'totes amazingballs'.

I shake my head again. Not a single wobble. Even so, I wind one final piece of tape round my phone and hair, shuddering to think of all the split ends this must be giving me. I do a few warm-up stretches to delay getting in the sea. Could that rock be getting further away? I need some motivation. As I stretch out my hamstrings, I imagine Reception Rock is a charity shop, and Kate Moss has just dropped off four bin bags. Inside the bags is stuff she's never even cut the labels off. The charity-shop lady hasn't got a clue and prices each bag at a pound. I have to get to that fantasy-charity-shop-really-a-rock *now*!

Pumped up with thoughts of Dior and Galliano, I march into the sea, wade out to my waist, then start a strong (yet cautious) breaststroke. I keep my head stuck high out of the water. After five minutes of swimming, I turn round to check out how far I've come. Not bad. And I didn't scream once getting in. Maybe Stråla's toughening me up, or maybe I only scream when someone's watching.

I swim on, my head stuck out of the water like a periscope. Soon my arms start to ache, but I don't slow down. *Fendi*, I think . . . *text from Betty . . . Chanel . . . Facebook . . . Instagram . . . photo of Bea's sister doing something weird . . . you can do it, Kat!*

By the time I touch Reception Rock, my legs feel like spaghetti. It's hard climbing out of the sea because the rock is so slippery and the only way I can get up is by lying on my stomach and wriggling forward like a seal (definitely not like a mermaid).

When I finally haul myself out, I lie still for a few seconds, getting my breath back and enjoying the sensation of the warm rock on my body. Then I notice the rock is *covered* in crusty bird poo and I am so up. The rock is a metre wide, so I find a tiny poo-free space and sit in it, legs crossed. Carefully, I ease my phone out of the tape, take a deep breath and then turn it on.

I stare at the screen.

Nothing.

Not one single bar of reception! I groan. Reception Rock? *Rubbish Swedish poo rock!* Suddenly, I'm overwhelmed with tiredness from my swim and my chest aches with disappointment. I'm such an idiot. Why did I believe this would work? 'Stupid phone!' I shout. 'You are useless and I'm going to chuck you in the sea!' And I nearly do, but then I remember it's an iPhone and it has an awesome case that looks like a bottle of Chanel nail varnish. It's the only present Britta has ever given me that I like. 'Today is your lucky day,' I say, giving it a shake.

Then, while I'm scowling at the screen, a single, beautiful, magical bar of perfect reception flickers on to the screen and my phone goes crazy with vibrating and pinging as message after message appears.

'Beautiful thing,' I say, kissing the screen. 'I'm sorry I said all those mean things to you.' Then, before I read anything, I send a message to Bea, Betty and Pearl just in case the reception goes: **Remember me? It's Kat, your lovely friend. I just swam about half a mile so I could send this to you! xxx Kat**

Almost immediately, I get one back from Pearl: **What do you want? A medal?**

Ignoring her, I send another message to all of them. **I have met Leo. Is he a Scandi God? Send me a letter and I will tell you! X**

Pearl: **Don't bother.**

Even Pearl's massive negativity can't ruin the friend-frenzy I'm on. I spend ten blissful minutes going through all the messages I've missed. From Bea, I discover that she's doing a Tango Boot Camp with her boyfriend, Ollie, and that Betty has started wearing a pastel blue furry moustache. Betty doesn't mention the tache, but she does tell me that Bea had an argument with Ollie after he tangoed with a 'slussy wearing white see-through jeggings'. Then Bea tells me tango 'was a bit complicated' so her and Ollie are sticking to jive.

Pearl's actually sent the most messages. Usually, they are rants about girls in our year and it's hard to keep up with who are her besties and who's a 'skank'. For example: **In chemist's with Tiann and she robbed an eyeshadow. Thought of you pinching smoothie!!! Ha. Gotta love Tiann cause She's MENTAL!! X Pearl.** Then, forty minutes later she sent: **Tiann and me had fight in Greggs. She wouldn't get me a sausage roll and I know she had £5. Cow. We got thrown out so HA TIANN DIDN'T GET HER DOUGHNUT HA HA HA!!! I hate her mean ass.** A few hours later, Pearl sends: **Tiann and me just rang Levi pretending to be YOU and asked him to meet up by the swings at the rec for 'fun'n'giggles'. He said 'no thanks' HA HA HA!!!!**

Levi Jordan blew me out? Unacceptable. I am *utterly* out of his league.

Suddenly, my phone beeps. It's a message from Betty! **So happy you're alive. Clearly you fancy Leo. Even**

120

thousands of miles away I can read your mind because it is so simple. x Betty

The girl's a clairvoyant. Quickly, I reply: **Anyone would fancy him. He is a genuine 9/10. I know I said that Frankie Pellett was a 9, but now I've met Leo, Frankie is demoted to a 7. In fact, Leo's turned my whole ranking system upside down. It's very confusing.**

Betty: **Oh my God. Frankie Pellett, a 7?!? Are you sure you've not got cabin fever? Maybe he looks like a troll (could he actually be a troll?) but you can't see it because you are currently boy-deprived! PS We've sent you a letter!**

Me: **Leo's no troll.**

Betty: **Evidence?**

Me: **My smile right now.** ☺

Betty: **You are so freakin adoraballs!**

Just as I'm replying that I've heard she's rocking some blue facial hair, the reception goes. I actually shake my phone to see if I can get it back. I stare at it. A second ago I was laughing with my friends; now

I'm on my own on a rock in the Baltic. But if I got reception once, I can get it again . . . Can't I? I hang around for five minutes, but nothing happens. Tomorrow I'll come out here again, and the day after that, and every single day until I can text my friends again. I will not give up!

Luckily, the tape is still sticky and my phone goes back into its Sellotape nest. I slip and slide back into the water and start to swim back to the island, my grinning head sticking straight out of the water.

Levi Jordan? Outrageous!

I go straight to the shop to see if there's a letter waiting for me. I avoid the paths and, instead, off-road through the forest. I think the Sellotape has done bad things to my forehead and I can't risk bumping into Leo.

After checking the *mötesplats* is clear, I dash into the shop. Before I ask about the letter, I get a bottle of water and a watermelon lolly out of the freezer cabinet. Then I have a brainwave. Obviously, the shop has electricity – it has fridges, freezers and a till. It must have its own generator. I follow the cable coming out of the back of the freezer until I find a plug socket . . . A plug socket! Such a beautiful sight. I wonder if I could plug my phone in for a while?

'Ah, Frida's niece,' calls out Juni. Guiltily, I stick my head out from the back of the freezer. She's holding a basket. 'You have a letter.' I know which is mine because only one letter is covered in heart-shaped stamps, foam stickers and glitter. Plus it's addressed to *Lady Kat Knightley of Fartington Manor*. It's the most gorgeous thing I have ever seen.

After checking the *mötesplats* again, I run back into the woods, clutching my letter, pink watermelon juice dripping on my legs. 'Kat!' a voice calls out. 'Wait for me.' Nanna comes running after me. For once, she's not wearing anything eccentric. In fact, she's wearing some serious running gear, which on her actually looks quite eccentric. 'I've been training with Sören for Tuff Troll,' she explains. 'He kept imitating me running.

Like this.' She runs ahead of me, her knees lifted high, her hands raised like a begging dog. She stops and waits for me to catch up. 'But I don't run like that, do I?'

'I don't think so. I've never really seen you run. Not properly.'

'OK. Watch this.' She does a quick sprint. Once again, her knees are high and she has begging hands.

'You look like you're pretending to be a horse,' I say, deciding to kick out the truth.

'Really?' She frowns and shrugs. 'I punched Sören and made him cry. Will you walk with me back to my cabin?' It's out of my way, but I'm starting to enjoy drifting around Stråla.

As I lick my lolly, Nanna explains her training schedule. Apparently, Otto fancies himself as a bit of a personal trainer because of his days spent in the Swedish Navy and has created a Tuff Troll regime for her and Sören. 'Tomorrow we have to run three times round the island,' she says.

'Maybe I'll join you,' I say. We're at the cabins by the youth hostel.

'Really?'

'No!' I give her a shove. 'I can't run.'

'Everyone can run.'

'Not me.'

'You're coming to the disco on Friday, aren't you?'

'Every Friday is disco night?'

'Except the one before Tuff Troll. Otto takes Tuff Troll very seriously.' Wow. Stråla loves a disco. Suddenly Nanna's eyes widen and she grabs my hands. 'Can we get ready together? That would be so totes amazeballing!'

'Amazeballs,' I say. 'OK, you come round to my place.'

'Yes!' she says, then she starts running, or should I say galloping, towards her cabin. 'Leo will be there,' she yells over her shoulder. 'He always helps Otto with the discos.' Then she whinnies and lets herself in.

A letter *and* a guaranteed Leo-moment on the horizon. Definitely *totes-amazeballing*.

I decide to take a shortcut home. On the way, I read my letter. I just can't wait.

Dear Kattingtons

Betty AND Bea here, although it's the Betty-Bomb in charge of writing. I'm round at Bea's house and we've been helping Emma make a model of a fried breakfast because we got inspired when we were watching Mr Maker. Bea's so lucky to have a little sister. Anyway, we decided to get a bit crafty with your letter too. Hope you like it!

In case you are worried about missing out on some mad summer action back here, allow me to repeat myself: we were watching MR MAKER. Seriously, you aren't missing a thing. Here is our main news:

Me:

★ Have been to Brighton with the sexiest boy on the planet. That's right, <u>my</u>

<u>boyfriend</u>, Bill. Still can't believe I have a boyfriend.

★ Argued several times with Dad over length of my hot pants. Didn't help myself when I said, 'But, Dad, they need to be short. Why do you think they are called <u>hot</u> pants and not <u>daggy</u> pants?'

★ Am about to go camping in Devon with Dad and Rue. Have allowed his GF to come on holiday with us on the condition that Bill is allowed to come for a few nights. Dad says Bill has to sleep in the tent with him, and Rue has to share with me!!! Both hilaire and horrific all at the same time.

Bea (it's Bea writing now, Kat, because I don't trust Betty):

★ Jived in the town centre with Ollie as part of WW2 Day. V embarrassing as some girls

127

from our year (including Pearl Harris) stood at the front sniggering. Pearl shouted out 'Jive-tastic!' loads of times in a sarcastic voice.

★ Made doughnuts. Not good. Looked like something Pinky might produce.

★ Went to Ollie's grandad's seventieth birthday party and Ollie sang 'Somewhere Over the Rainbow' for him. Despite this, I still fancy him!

Betty here again. While Bea was writing that I had a serious chat with Emma:

Emma: What's a baby monkey called?

Me: I don't know.

Emma: It must be something that rhymes with monkey . . . Is it a funky?

Once again, I wish I had a little sister who says funny things and wanders around in her pants. Hang on, I do: that's exactly what you do! You're my little sister, Kat.

Well, we miss you, Scandi-Kat, even though you've only been gone three days. Only twenty-nine to go!

Loads of love,

Beatty xxxxxxxxxxxxxxxxx

TEN

I read the letter twice, then put it back in the envelope. I've left a trail of sequins and glitter all through the woods.

I look around me. I've been so distracted that somehow I've managed to get lost. Below me I can see a path. Holding on to a branch, I try to scramble down the slope. Unfortunately, it turns out the branch isn't attached to a tree and my feet shoot out from under me and I start to slide down the hill, picking up speed as I go. I grab a passing rock, but I miss, spin round and tumble on to the path at the bottom with a painful bump.

I rub my head, then look up. This isn't a path – it's a garden, a garden that surrounds a tent. Leo's tent.

I know it's Leo's tent because he's standing a few feet in front of me, hanging out his washing in his pants. Well, this is starting to even things out a bit. He stares at me, a peg in one hand and a towel in the other. 'Hello,' I say, jumping to my feet. 'I just fell down a hill!'

'Are you OK?' In a flash he wraps the towel around his waist. 'You've got something in your hair.'

I pat my head. 'Oh, that? It's just where leaves and stuff have stuck to the Sellotape . . .' I start to pull out twigs and pine needles. 'How do I get back to the path? I think I'm lost.'

'Over there,' says Leo, pointing.

'Great!' I say. 'Thanks.' I start to walk away, trying hard to hold my head high.

'Kat,' Leo calls out. 'Your head is bleeding.'

'Oh.'

'And I've got plasters. Also, I was just about to have some coffee . . .'

'*Fika?*' I turn round. Thank you, *fika*, you wonderful tradition!

131

'I haven't got any cake, just some chocolate.' Still holding the towel with one hand, Leo throws a last T-shirt on the line and pegs it in place.

'What kind?'

'Plopp.'

'Thank you, I mean, yes, please.' Trying not to smile too much, I go back into the little garden. 'I'd love to have some coffee and Plopp with you . . . and maybe a plaster.'

Soon, Leo and I are sitting in deckchairs and drinking coffee on his 'veranda' – a big flat rock that faces the sea. 'This is the only tent I've ever seen that has a garden and mail box,' I say.

'My grandad used to own some land here.' Leo passes me another square of Plopp. 'He sold most of it, but kept this bit for us to come camping. I like to spend the whole summer here. Mum and Dad come out for a couple few weeks.'

'My mum and dad would never trust me to stay on my own. Isn't it spooky at night?'

'I like it. It's very quiet. During the day, I sit here and watch the birds in the juniper tree. They don't even know I'm here.'

'Let's try it,' I say. 'Don't talk.' We sit in silence and stare at the tree. Occasionally, I glance at Leo, but only for a moment. He's got dressed now, and he's sitting cross-legged in his deckchair, his chin resting on his hands. For a few minutes, nothing happens, then little birds appear out of nowhere, too many to count, and they hop around from branch to branch doing their birdy thing. I take a sip of my coffee and they vanish with a flutter of tiny wings. 'Sorry,' I say. 'My bad. Noisy sip.'

'They'll be back.' Leo sits back in his deckchair and looks at me. 'So, why are you staying here with Frida? Where are your mum and dad?'

'Well. That's a long story.'

'Tell me.' He looks at his watch. It's the big water-proof type. 'I've got until tomorrow evening.'

'You made another joke! Like the Starbucks one. I like your jokes.'

'I can do more jokes in Swedish,' he says and he smiles. It's amazing what strange things a smile can do to your tummy. Maybe it's the smile, or the peaceful view, or maybe it's the strong coffee, but something makes me mega chatty, and I find myself telling Leo everything. I tell him about the Marks and Spencer's smoothie, Britta's parents' evening and Joel. I even tell him about Dad's gross shorts.

And then, I don't know why, but I talk about other things, things I haven't really told anyone before. Like how I never see my family on Saturdays because they always do triathlons and races together, even on my birthday, and how Britta and I used to watch cartoons on Saturday morning, both of us in our PJs, lounging on the sofa. Then I tell him how Mum has framed six of Britta's pictures from playgroup, but only two of mine. 'It doesn't matter,' I say. 'Mum just ran out of space on the wall – Britta does a lot of things that need framing – but there was this one picture I did, a portrait of Mum made of pasta, that was *really* good and definitely better than Britta's potato-print train. Mum left it on the kitchen table until all the pasta fell off.'

'Perhaps it was too chunky to frame,' says Leo.

'I did use spinach spirals for her hair, but somehow they always find room for Britta's trophies and medals.'

'Well, my mum and dad never framed any of my pictures. As soon as I brought them home, they recycled them . . . and I'm an only child.'

'Maybe you're embarrassingly rubbish at art.'

He laughs. 'Possibly. But I think it's more that they didn't realise that parents are supposed to get excited by what their kids do, even if they have to fake it. My mum and dad are quite . . .' He frowns up at the juniper tree. 'Distracted. You know, by their jobs.'

Leo tells me all about his family and friends, and what school is like in Sweden. Soon *fika* becomes lunch and while Leo makes us sandwiches, I take a tour of the tent. It's neat and pretty and feels more like a cabin than a tent. It has two separate bedrooms and a proper kitchen, rugs, herbs growing on the window sill and even a guitar. 'That's my dad's,' Leo says. 'You can play the guitar. Why don't you play something?'

'OK,' I say. I take the guitar outside and start to tune it. Inside, Leo is clattering plates and whistling. As I pluck each string in turn, a brown bird – Leo would know what it is – lands by my feet and stares up at me, head tilted to one side. I'm shaded by trees and beams of sunlight creep through the leaves. One of these beams falls on the bird. I run through a few scales and then start playing a Spanish song that matches the sunshine. The bird carries on watching me with its beady black eyes. There's a moment's silence after I pluck the last notes. 'Did you like it?' I ask the bird.

Leo puts a sandwich on the floor next to me and the bird flies away. '*Det var vackert*,' he says. *It was beautiful*. My cheeks go pink.

'Thank you . . . Those sandwiches look *vackra*.'

'They're just cheese.'

'I'm very hungry.'

I don't go home after lunch. A couple of times I get up, but then we start talking again, or I play another song, or the chessboard comes out. Of course, I don't want to go. I could stay here forever, studying Leo's face and listening to him talk about nuthatches and tree pipits and his obsession with all things non-human. Leo is particularly into whales and he tells me all sorts of crazy things about them, like how they can suffocate if they accidentally swallow a bird and that killer whales are actually big dolphins . . . killer dolphins!

Somehow, I end up cutting Leo's hair. He keeps blowing it out of his eyes, so he gets some scissors and starts to snip away at it, telling me this is how he cuts it in the summer. It's painful watching how badly he does it, so I take over. His hair is warm from the sun. I know this because I run my fingers through it way more times than I need to. 'There,' I say, cutting off a final strand and messing it up. 'Finished.'

A spluttering engine makes us both turn round. Otto appears on his scooter and stops by the tent. Leo jumps to his feet. '*Hej!*' Otto says. He seems surprised to see me here. Leo goes over and helps him unload a cylinder of gas. 'That should be enough for now,' Otto says in Swedish. He glances at me. 'I'll collect the used one later.'

'*Tack*,' says Leo, folding his arms.

Otto turns to me. 'I'm going to your cabin next,' he says in English. 'Do you want a lift?'

'Oh.' I look at Leo. 'Well –'

'No thanks,' says Leo. 'We're going for a swim.'

Are we? Great! I turn back to Otto, trying and failing to hide my huge smile. 'Can you tell Frida that I'll be back later?'

He glances at Leo then back at me. 'Of course,' he says.

Together we watch as Otto drives up the path and the sound of the engine fades away. Somehow, Otto has burst the magic bubble that surrounded us. Leo starts to tidy up the plates and cups that are lying around and carries them inside. 'Are you sure you don't want me to go?' I say. Suddenly, I feel like I might have stayed too long.

Leo sticks his head out of the tent. 'No. I don't want you to go, Kat.'

'So, are we going swimming?'

'Not yet,' he says. 'It needs to be dark. I want to show you something. It's something even more *vackra* than the cheese sandwich.'

When the sky is inky blue and the sun has almost set, Leo and I walk down a path that leads to the sea. There's no beach, just a pile of smooth grey rocks.

'We need to go in just here,' Leo says, tapping the edge of a rock. 'It's not slippery.'

'OK,' I say, pulling my dress over my head, glad that it's shadowy. For some reason we're whispering. While we waited for it to get dark, Leo made pasta and I played the entire *Frozen* soundtrack on the guitar. Leo sang along, which was funny, until we both sang 'Love is an Open Door' and it suddenly got awkward.

We leave our clothes on the rock and slip into the water. Leo goes first and I follow. My feet sink into weed and the water makes me gasp. 'Follow me,' says Leo. We swim side by side. The water is dark and deep and I can't even see my hands moving.

'The moon is disappearing,' I say. 'Frida said this would happen. It's called a dark moon.'

'That's even better.'

'For what?'

Leo stops swimming. We face each other and we tread water. 'This,' he says. He waves his hand through the sea. On the surface, slipping through his fingers, are thousands of tiny neon lights, sparkling as if they are alive.

I gasp. I try to pick some up, but the green sparks just slip through my fingers. I kick my feet and a cloud of light bursts around me like fireworks. I laugh. 'What is it?'

'Phosphorescence.' Leo turns round in the sea and he's surrounded in a swirl of colour. 'Heatless light generated by marine organisms.'

'Nope. It's definitely magic,' I say. 'Probably something to do with mermaids.' I lift one arm out of the water and the luminous specks cling to my skin. 'Or it could be fairies.'

'Or chemicals.'

'More likely it's fairies.' I try to catch a handful. I think I'm starting to believe in magic.

'It's in your hair,' says Leo. He reaches towards me then drops his hand. We stare at each other. 'Beautiful, isn't it?'

I nod. The sky above us is vast and starry and just two feet of glittery sea separate us. More than anything I want to swim into his arms. I hardly dare to breathe. Something should happen now, but I need Leo to make it happen. If only the crab from *The Little Mermaid* could pop out of the sea and start singing 'Kiss the Girl'.

But Sebastian doesn't make an appearance – that would be too much magic for one night. Instead, Leo says, 'You're getting cold. Let's go back.' Then he turns and starts to swim towards the shore.

I am cold. Shivering, I follow Leo through the fading phosphorescence. I can't stop thinking that something has just changed and Leo is drifting away from me again, like he did when we came back from Vilda. I push the thought away. He just spent the *whole* day with me. He cooked me pasta! It's just that when I'm with Leo, life feels different to anything I've ever felt before. It's like phosphorescence: too amazing to believe and impossible to hold on to.

We pull ourselves back up on the rocks and dry off. I put on my dress and feel in the pocket to check my letter from Bea and Betty is still there. 'Shall I walk you back to your cabin?' asks Leo.

'I'm fine. It's not that far.' I want to think about today, about every moment.

'Perhaps I will see you tomorrow?' He says this quickly, like he's embarrassed. He pulls his towel round his shoulders. 'I'm going back to Stockholm on Saturday, just for one day, but except for that, I'm around most days.'

'I'd like to see you tomorrow.' Clearly, this is a massive understatement. 'And thank you for the pasta . . . and the plaster,' I say. 'That rhymes!' *Shut up, Kat*, wave and leave. I force myself to turn round. 'And the Plopp!' I call over my shoulder.

Then I walk across the island, and I think about everything: every smile, every word and every glitter of phosphorescence. It happened, and I never, ever want to forget it.

ELEVEN

'Ahh! Look at Otto,' says Nanna. 'He's totes adoreballs.'

'*Adorbs*, and enough with the totes, Nanna . . . but, yes, he does look cute.' Otto has set up his disco in a corner of the cafe and he's put on his smiley face waist-coat again. The Friday night disco's much smaller than Solsken, but the cafe's still buzzing. Nanna and I are sitting round one of the rocks that sticks up through the decking making a lumpy and very impractical table. We're sharing some fries which taste amazeballs. They should do, they cost nearly five pounds.

The sea is a spectacular blue and so still that every tree, rock and boat has its mirror image reflected perfectly in the water. The evening sun and Otto's ambient tunes add to the magical atmosphere, as does the knowledge that any minute now, Leo will turn up. We've spent the past three days together, almost every moment. I've helped him paint the fence round his tent, we've kayaked around the island, swum, eaten loads of ice cream, but most of all we've spent hours hanging out at the cafe and talking. It's been amazing . . . Except for the lack of kissing, but surely that will change tonight.

'You look pretty,' says Nanna. 'Like a sunflower.'

'Tall and droopy?'

'No! You know what I mean.'

'Big head?'

'No. You stand out.'

'Thanks.' I look down at my yellow dress. Compared to the holidaymakers, I've clearly made an effort. Everyone else is in shorts and flip-flops. It took me ages to decide what to wear tonight.

'And your hair looks cool. You look like thingy from *The Hunger Games*.'

Instinctively, I touch my plait. When we were getting ready, Nanna couldn't believe how I could do my hair without using a mirror. I had to explain that back at school, I have four hours of maths a week and a teacher on the verge of a nervous breakdown. This gives me plenty of time to practise plaiting techniques.

Sören sits down with us. He's holding a massive ice cream. 'Otto says he wants us to work on our front crawl tomorrow,' he tells Nanna, ignoring me as usual. 'Oh, and he wanted me to tell you that your face looks like a cowpat.'

'Shut up.'

'A fresh cowpat . . .'

'Shut up!'

'. . . from an ugly cow.'

'SHUT UP!' Nanna hits the bottom of the cone so that ice cream splodges all over his face and glasses.

'Don't care,' he says, leaving the smeared ice cream where it is.

'*Hej!*' a voice calls out, a voice that manages to be deep and gentle all at the same time. I look up. Leo is walking towards us. He's wearing khaki shorts and a crumpled shirt and his brown-blond hair is as tangled and sea-styled as it was when I first saw him. I don't think my hair cut has made any difference. He looks totally and utterly *right*. My heart does a somersault.

'Leo!' Nanna leaps up and throw her arms around him.

'Hello,' he says, laughing. He glances down at me and smiles. Immediately, I blush.

'I hope you've been in training,' says Sören, quickly wiping the ice cream off his face. 'Nanna and I are going to beat you in Tuff Troll this year.' The moment he finishes speaking, Nanna hits the cone again, shrieking with laughter. '*Dumbom!*' Sören tries to stick the ice cream in her face.

'Don't be so rude to Kat,' she says. 'Speak in *English*.'

'Sorry,' Sören says to me.

'That's OK. I know what a *dumbom* is.'

'It's Nanna,' he says.

Leo sits next to me, so close our shoulders are almost touching. 'They've been like this since I first met them when they were five,' he tells me.

'And you were so grown up and *eight*,' says Nanna. 'Actually, you were almost entirely grown up when you were eight.' I try not to stare at Leo's toffee-coloured hair or the way it curls by his ears, or the manly way he grips his bottle of lingonberry juice. I try not to stare, but I fail, and it's impossible not to meet his eyes. Nanna saves us from an awkward situation by saying, 'Awks. Why's no one speaking?'

'We are,' I say quickly. 'I love your eyes, Leo.' Shirt. SHIRT! I meant to say *shirt*. Oh, God.

'Thanks,' he says, laughing.

Then Nanna really does save us from a truly awkward situation by shouting, '"Happyland"!' And jumping to her feet. 'Who's going to dance with me?'

I look at the empty dance floor. 'But no one's dancing,' I say. 'Not even the children.'

148

'Seriously, Nanna,' says Sören, ' "*Happyland*"?'

'I just love it.' She's jiggling around on the spot. 'Please!'

'I'll dance with you,' says Leo. He gets up, takes her by the hand like she's Cinderella and leads her on to the tiny dance floor. Then they start to dance, *properly* dance. Leo twirls her under his arm and everything. Soon they're surrounded by children who tug them apart, hold on to their hands and make them dance in a huge circle.

Leo didn't want to dance, but he did. He did it for Nanna. 'Come on, Sören,' I say, getting to my feet.

'No way,' he says, putting the last bit of cone into his mouth. Then he sighs and stands up, tugging his T-shirt down. 'Alright,' he says, 'but this is all my *dumbom* sister's fault.'

Soon, the sun is setting, and I am jumping up and down with a little girl called Moa. Another song I've never heard of comes on, but I don't care and neither does Moa. Leo and Nanna's waltz goes badly wrong and Sören is standing on a rock. He might be dancing, or he might be pretending to be a robot. Hard to tell. '*Snabbare!*' shouts Moa. *Faster!*

'Hold on!' I say, then I pull her round so fast she screams with delight. I look over at Leo and he's watching me. This time neither of us look away. I'm in happyland.

After the next song, we go back to the rock. Most of the children are dragged off to bed and, all around us, tea lights glitter on the tables. Nanna starts reminiscing about the old days. Apparently, one legendary summer, Leo wore denim cut-offs that his mum had sown Lisa Simpson patches on. He shakes his head. 'It was Bart.'

'Doesn't make it any better,' I say.

'At least he wasn't being a punk,' Sören says. 'Last year, Nanna was a punk and the year before that she was a goth.'

'But I found wearing black too hot,' she says.

Otto puts on 'Lovefool' by The Cardigans, and when the chorus starts the four of us join in. I look around. No one in the cafe seems to mind.

And that's when I see her. A girl wearing shorts and boots is walking straight towards us, her perfect blonde hair swinging from side to side. A delicate gold chain with a swirling 'P' rests on her chest. She crouches down just behind Leo, wraps her fingers over his eyes and puts her mouth close to his ear. '*Gissa vem?*' she says. *Guess who?* Her nails are shell-pink and her hair falls over Leo's shoulder.

He puts his fingers on hers. For a moment he doesn't speak, then he says 'Peeta?' Nanna's eyes grow wide and I stare, confused.

'I managed to come early,' she whispers into his ear.

Leo sits there, his fingers still resting on hers, and time stands still. My heart thuds in my chest. 'But . . . you weren't supposed to be coming until the race,' he says, pulling down her hands. He stares up at her then jumps to his feet. 'Sorry, I mean –' But he doesn't finish his sentence because Peeta slips her arms round his waist and kisses him. On the lips. *Peeta* not *Peter*. I feel like I've been punched in the stomach.

Leo steps back but his hand rests on her shoulder and the pain inside me grows stronger. Quickly, he says, 'This is my friend, Peeta.'

'Girlfriend!' she says, slapping him playfully on the tummy. 'You're so shy, Leo.' She smiles at each of us in turn. She has a single dimple on her left cheek and her hair is spun gold. She looks like an angel.

Nanna leans towards me. 'Amazeboobs,' she whispers. 'Is that right?'

'Yes,' I say. 'That's right.' Peeta's wearing a very tight vest. She's amaze-*everything*.

'Where are you staying?' Leo asks.

'The youth hostel. I'm lucky they had a free bed because of a cancellation, so I've booked it until after Tuff Troll.'

'OK,' says Leo, nodding. They sit down together and Peeta tells us about her journey and her run for the ferry. 'If I hadn't been in training for Tuff Troll, I might not have made it.' Leo has been staring at the ground, but he glances up at me. I turn away and pretend to be fascinated by the sunset. 'Lovefool' is still playing. I stare and stare at the sunset until I stop wanting to cry. Why didn't he tell me he had a girlfriend? Or have I been imagining everything that's happened over the past few days? When the phosphorescence swirled round us under the stars, was he thinking about *her*?

I force myself to turn back and smile and laugh at everything Peeta says – refusing to look at Leo – and generally I act like I couldn't care less that he's got a girlfriend. I'm a good actor. Soon, I've learnt a lot about her. Somehow, all our conversations come back to the topic of Peeta and how awesome she is.

'I love that you two are twins,' she tells Sören and Nanna. 'There's a town in Brazil where eight per cent of the population are twins. I went there last year with my mum and we worked with street children. We travelled around afterwards. It helped my Portuguese *and* my football. Those kids know how to kick a ball!' She says all this in perfect English with a slight American accent from her time 'spent in the States', and she uses

English words I don't even know. She loves the 'irides-cence' of the sea and says I look 'resplendent' in my dress. Is this a compliment? I'm not sure. Suddenly, I hate sitting here in my yellow dress. I wish I could disappear.

Otto puts on a dance track and comes over to us. He stands looking down at us, arms folded. His eyes flick from me to Peeta, taking everything in, and I have the terrible feeling that he knew about Peeta and that she was coming out here. Peeta beams up at him. 'What gave you the idea of starting Tuff Troll?' she asks.

'You've all heard of Ö Till Ö?'

Everyone nods, except me. I'm finding it hard to concentrate on anything right now. 'It's one of the world's toughest endurance races and it happens right here in the archipelago.' He slaps his big hand down on our rock. 'Contestants race in pairs, swimming between twenty-four islands. When they get to an island, they climb out of the water and run. Ten kilometres of swimming and sixty-five kilometres of running. All in one day.' His eyes grow wide. 'I kept seeing all these fat lazy teenagers turning up at the island and eating fries and drinking fizzy stuff –' He pauses here. I'm sipping my Coke and my straw is making big slurpy noises. 'So I started Tuff Troll. It's just a bit of fun: a kilometre of swimming and kayaking, and five or so kilometres of running.'

'I can't wait,' says Peeta.

'In three weeks,' Otto says, staring at us each in turn, 'we will discover who are the toughest trolls on Stråla!' Suddenly he scowls. 'Song's ending,' he says, walking off. Peeta starts to describe her unusual, but excellent sea-swimming technique.

Out of nowhere, Leo says, 'Kat's good at the crawl.'

Everyone looks at me. Peeta narrows her eyes. It's just for a moment – no one else notices – then she smiles and says, 'Are you entering Tuff Troll, Kat?'

'No. I'm that lazy sort of teenager. I'll sit on this rock, eat fries and drink Coke, and watch you guys doing it.'

Peeta shrugs. 'I guess it's not for everyone.' Then she rests her arm across Leo's back. 'Also,' she says, 'you don't have anyone to enter with, do you?'

For a moment, no one speaks. Everyone noticed *that*. She looks at me innocently. 'You're right,' I say. 'I definitely can't enter.'

'Do you think you could do it? I mean, if you did have someone to race with?'

'Probably not,' I say. Leo stares at his empty juice bottle and picks at the label.

'Yes you could!' cries Nanna, nudging me.

'It's a tough race.' Peeta shrugs. 'You have to be fit and focused.' I bet when Peeta was little she used to pinch people. I've hardly spoken since she arrived, but somehow she knows how to get at me. 'Hey,' she says, turning to Leo and smiling brightly. 'Will you show me the boats?' She pulls him to his feet. As he walks away, he glances back at me, but I look away.

Sören, Nanna and I sit in silence for a moment. 'I'm getting a drink,' says Sören. 'Anyone want one?' I shake

156

my head. He shrugs and walks off, leaving me and Nanna alone. Together we watch as Peeta and Leo walk towards the harbour.

After a moment, Nanna says, 'I'm sorry, Kat. I didn't know he had a girlfriend.'

'Forget it,' I say, shrugging. 'We're just friends. It doesn't matter.' Like I said, I'm a good actor. I turn to her. 'How about a game of chess?'

Nanna reaches for her rucksack. 'Are you sure?'

'Yes! Nothing says Friday night like a game of chess.' I force myself to smile brightly, but inside, my heart is aching so much I want to curl up. After I've beaten Nanna – she lets me win – I say I'm going back to the cabin. I can't fake happy for another moment.

To get into the woods I have to walk past Leo and Peeta, who are sitting on the harbour wall. Peeta's waving her hands around in an animated way, probably describing how she saved the life of a street child by doing an awesome tackle. I speed up, keen to get past them. Then, out of nowhere, I hear Peeta say my name.

157

'*Har du tillbringat hela dagen med Kat?*' she says. I can tell from her voice that she's angry. Immediately, I translate her words: *You spent the whole day with Kat?*

I'm frozen to the spot. For a moment, Leo doesn't say anything, then he puts his arm round her. She shrugs him off. 'Was it fun?' Peeta asks.

He doesn't reply, so she nudges him and asks him again. He sighs and says, '*Det betydde ingenting, hen.*' *It meant nothing.* Then he tells Peeta that I screamed whenever a drop of water touched me and that all I cared about was getting a tan. I feel cold and sick, but I can't move. I stand and listen, my hand resting on the papery bark of a tree.

Peeta laughs. '*Hon är blåst!*' she says. *She's an airhead. Dumb.*

And Leo says *nothing*. He just puts his arm back round Peeta and pulls her to him. I wait and I watch, but he leaves those words hanging in the air. He might as well have said them himself. In a second, everything that's happened over the past week – moon-bathing, kayaking to Vilda, even watching birds in the juniper tree – disappears on the sea breeze and becomes *nothing*. Behind me, the laughter and music fade away and the ache inside me burns and turns into something else.

How *dare* he?

Without thinking, I march forward. '*Hej!*' I shout. They spin round. Peeta puts her hand over her mouth, but it doesn't hide her smile. Leo looks horrified. Quickly, he pulls his arm away from Peeta. 'I just came to let you both know I've changed my mind.' I see my hands are shaking, so I cross my arms.

'About what?' Peeta asks.

'Tuff Troll. I am going to enter. One of my friends is coming over – she's pretty fit, actually – she's coming to stay and we're going to compete. I just wanted to let you know and say . . .'

'Yes?' says Peeta gently, like she's talking to child.

But I ignore her and look at Leo. 'That I *do* have someone.' Then I spin round and walk away.

'Kat!' Leo calls, but I don't hang around to hear what he has to say. A huge childish sob is rising up inside me. I have to get into the forest. I don't want Leo to ever know that he made me cry. I don't want Leo to ever know that he ever made me feel *anything*.

I hate him, I think, as I brush away my tears. I don't like Peeta, but I *hate* Leo. How could I have got him so wrong? Somehow, I have to get one of my friends out here. With Betty or Bea by my side, I can hold my head high, enter the race and prove that I'm not someone he can laugh at.

Because I'm not an airhead – I'm strong.

I was strong enough to jump off a cliff when my legs were shaking, strong enough to come to this island in the middle of nowhere without my family and I'm definitely strong enough to enter their stupid troll race.

TWELVE

The next morning, I write a letter to my friends.

Dear Beatty

   I need one of you to come to Sweden.
Now.

   I'm <u>serious</u>.

   I got Leo all wrong. He forgot to mention
he has a girlfriend, Peeta, and she turned
up on the island today. I can't even begin
to describe how I feel about Leo right now.
A lot of things happened tonight and somehow
I announced that one of my amazing friends
was going to come over to Sweden and

enter Tuff Troll with me. This was a lie, but I desperately need it to be true.

Who wants to be a Tuff Troll? Betty does ... Bea does!

Please, please, please, please. My auntie says it's cool for one of you to come over here (or even both of you!?) and you won't have to pay for the travel because Mum and Dad will. You know what fitness freaks they are. Me entering Tuff Troll will be a dream come true for them. Here's what you need to do:

★ Fly to Stockholm airport

★ Get the shuttle train to the city

★ Walk to the harbour (follow the signs)

★ Get 3 p.m. boat to Strála (the red one)
Simples! In three days, I'll go to the dock every day to see if one of you is on the boat. Which you definitely will be. I'm putting Mum's credit card details at the bottom of

the letter. I'm pretty sure this is breaking some law. Her security code is our phone number and her memorable word is Britta (natch). Please don't go on a spending spree with this card!!!

I know this seems mad, but it would be madly wonderful if one of you could come here and race with me.

Fingers, legs and toes crossed,

Kat xxxxxx

I add the credit card details then put the letter in an envelope. I address it to Bea just in case Betty's already gone camping. I'm just about to seal the envelope when I have an idea. I take the letter out and get another piece of paper. I copy it out, almost word for word, but this time I write Pearl's name at the top.

Pearl smokes like a chimney and I'm not even sure she can swim, but surely she's better than no one? I am a bit anxious about giving her Mum's card details, but before I know it, I've added them and I'm sealing the envelopes.

I find Frida in the kitchen staring into a swirling cup of coffee. She looks up with a huge smile. If it's actually possible, Beardy-beady has made Frida even happier than she was before. 'Where are you going?' she asks.

'For a run,' I say. 'I need to get fit if I'm going to enter Tuff Troll.'

'You're serious about that?' Frida's smile vanishes. Last night, when I got in, I asked her if a friend could come and stay, and then I told her that Leo's girlfriend had turned up. I didn't say anything else, I didn't need to. My red eyes told her everything. She tried to get me to talk, but I told her I was tired and went straight to bed.

Frida puts down her coffee cup and comes over to me. 'You don't need to prove anything, Kat.'

'I am going to enter the race, Frida.'

'Look . . . who cares if Leo's got a girlfriend?'

'It's not about that.' I bend down and tighten my laces.

Frida sighs. 'And you really think one of your friends will be allowed to come here on their own?' She puts her hand on my shoulder. 'Because it's a long way to come to help a friend out.'

I look at the letters. 'They're good friends. The best,' I say. 'One of them will come.' I'm not sure who I'm trying to convince.

'Well, great!' She gives me a hopeful smile. 'Well done for going running and . . . everything. You look very spotty.'

'Sporty?'

'No, spotty. I like your crazy shorts.' I don't have the right gear, but I've got trainers and shorts. What else do I need? Admittedly, my trainers are pastel pink and have never been used for any type of training, and my shorts are the red spotty ones I wear to bed, more boxers really. OK, they are boxers. A pair of Dad's that shrunk in the wash, but from a distance they look like shorts.

'I'm going to run to the shop, post my letters, then run back round the island.'

'Take care. And don't push yourself too hard.'

'I'm only going for a run, Frida,' I say as I jog out. 'How hard can it be?'

Hard! Very, very hard and horrible and pukey and hurty.

At first, I think running is great. I bounce into the woods and along the path. *Why don't I always run?* It's quicker than walking and I feel like I'm a kick-ass heroine in an action film. Filled with energy, I jump over logs and leap round roots. Then, after about four minutes, I get a stitch and soon every step I take sends a dart of pain into my waist. Action heroes don't say, 'Ow, ow, ow,' as they run, and they don't want to puke, do they? Sweat drips off my forehead and my heart thunders in my chest. I slow down but it still hurts, so I slow down a bit more. If anything, the pain increases.

Out of nowhere, an old lady overtakes me. She's walking. '*Hej!*' she calls as she disappears round the bend. I glance down at my feet. Those are *walking* feet. I'm not even running! What's the matter with me? I can dance; why can't I run?

I limp the rest of the way to the shop and post my letters. Then I stand outside the shop looking left and then right. I could just give up for the day, or I could carry on 'running' round the island. The problem is, my entire body is shouting: *Go home, Kat, lie down, DON'T EVER RUN AGAIN!*

Then I see Peeta and Leo.

They're sitting in the cafe. Peeta's sipping a cup of coffee and Leo's reading a book. Peeta sees me and smiles. But it's not a 'Hey there!' smile. It's an 'Oh dear. Look what *it's* doing now!' smile. It hits me like a slap in the face. Then Leo glances up. When he sees me, he pushes his chair back.

Immediately, I lift my head up high and start to run. And I mean *run*. Like a dog is chasing me. Now my entire body is shouting: *You can do it, Kat. Ignore the pain and embrace the burn!* My stitch has gone, but it's still agony. Somehow pride keeps me going.

I run through the campsite and along the coastal path. As I pass Otto's rental place, he looks up from the kayak he's sanding down. 'Chin up!' he shouts.

'What?' I turn to look at him and stumble over a root.

'Look forward!' he yells, and within moments he's alongside me, a streak of yellow and blue in his mustard running shorts and 'Ö Till Ö' T-shirt. 'Keep your shoulders still and run tall.' He actually pulls my shoulders back. 'Don't slouch, Kat.'

'You sound like my dad,' I gasp.

'Stop talking and get in the zone.'

'I don't have a zone . . . Unless my zone is a wanting-to-puke zone.'

'Breathe through your mouth and slow it down. Breathe deep, right to your stomach. Get that oxygen into your body.' I do what he says. I sound like Darth Vader having an asthma attack. Gradually, the nausea fades. 'Breathe in, *two, three, four*, release, *two, three*, *four*,' Otto says, repeating this again and again, until my breathing matches his words.

We pass a few campers, and then the posh cabins on the south of the island. At one point, we run next to the sea and I see Nanna and Sören swimming side by side, their identical heads bobbing up and down. Nanna spots me. 'Go Kat!' she yells. 'Work her lazy ass, Otto!'

'Idiot,' he mutters, then he abandons me and starts to boss the twins around instead. 'Face down, arms close to your ears. You two look like twin fools! What're you doing?'

My feet plod on automatically. Breathe, *two, three, four*, release, *two, three, four*. Sweat trickles down my back and my cheeks are on fire. Suddenly, I'm back at our cabin. How did I get here? Wow . . . I actually found the zone! I slow down, feeling hugely pleased with myself, but then a voice calls out, 'Pick up those lazy legs, pull back your shoulders and breathe!'

Otto appears by my side, blocking my escape route. Amazingly, I start doing another circuit of the island. My feet are obeying Otto and not *me*, their owner! 'Now,' Otto says, 'let's stretch it out.' He speeds up, and I speed up too. Are we racing? Yes! I'm racing an old man and he is so beating me. As we get closer to the cafe my heart starts to beat even faster, but I don't stop running. Leo and Peeta aren't going to make me stop doing anything.

Otto bursts into the *mötesplats* ahead of me, then pauses, waiting for me to catch up. I follow him, eyes flicking from the cafe to the shop, but Leo and Peeta are nowhere to be seen. My heart slows, but only fractionally. We jog on together all the way back to his hut.

'Now, walk for two minutes,' he says, 'then run for two. Keep that up all the way back to your cabin. That's your training for today.' He peels away from me, picks up his sandpaper and gets back to work. He isn't even out of breath.

Huh. Otto's training me. How did that happen? Obediently, I start to walk. 'Chin up!' Otto's voice follows me through the trees. 'And stand tall, girl, don't slouch!' He can't even see me . . . but I was slouching.

★

My warm-down is collapsing on to a mattress that Frida's dragged outside for sunbathing purposes. Blood roars in my ears and my heart pounds like it's trying to escape. 'Maybe I'll just put a towel under you,' says Frida.

Oh, and I'm sweating. A lot. I roll on my side, then roll back on to the towel she's spread out. 'Think . . . I might . . . die,' I whisper.

'Here.' She passes me a bottle of water. I lift my head up just enough to slurp some down. 'Your chakra is glowing,' she says. Then she laughs. 'You're actually purple, Kat. How do you feel?'

I stare at the sky. Clouds race past and whispering branches sway in the wind. I feel desperately hurt by what Leo said and did, and painfully jealous of Peeta. But I feel something else too. The sky spins slightly and my blood roars through my body. 'Alive,' I say.

THIRTEEN

Over the next few days, my life falls into a routine of running with Nanna, swimming to and from Reception Rock and avoiding Leo and Peeta. I actually incorporate this into my fitness regime. If I see one of them, I sprint off into the woods, trying to get as far away from them as possible. Everything aches: my muscles and my heart. My muscles feel better each morning, but the ache in my chest just won't go away.

The *mötesplats* is the real Leo/Peeta danger zone and I avoid it as much as possible, but soon my monstrous addiction to cinnamon buns forces me to risk a trip to Juni's shop.

The delicious smell of cinnamon, sugar and butter

tells me that she's just made a new batch and soon I'm leaving the shop, my nose buried in a paper bag.

A sigh makes me look up. Peeta's standing waiting to get past me, hands on her hips. For a second we look at each other, then she says, 'You've got sugar on your nose.' Quickly, I brush it off. Peeta doesn't look quite as amazeboobs as she did when she arrived. She looks tired and her hair is scraped back with a hairband. She glances over her shoulder and tucks a strand of hair behind her ear.

'Are you going in?' I ask, holding the door open.

She nods. 'I need an energy drink. Leo and I just kayaked to Fejan. We took a camping stove and he made me pancakes.' She watches me closely. I don't say a word. I know what she thinks about me. I'm not about to have a friendly chat with her. 'I see you've been running.' Peeta looks at my candy-pink trainers and smiles.

I manage a nod.

'OK . . . well, see you around!' Peeta walks into the

shop, saying '*Hej*, Juni,' like they are best friends. I let the door slam shut behind her.

I breathe deeply and stare at my bag. Peeta's made me feel sick. I can't go back to the cabin yet – I need to calm down. I decide to take a walk round the island.

As I pass Otto's cabin, he pops up from behind a stack of kayaks and calls out, 'Help me with this, Kat.' He's not the sort of person you argue with, so I go over. He holds out a bucket and sponge. With a sigh, I put down the bag with my cinnamon bun in it and take the frothy bucket.

'What do you want me to do?'

'Help Leo clean the roof of my cabin. It's covered in pigeon poop.'

What? I look up, and there, sitting on the tin roof of Otto's hut, is Leo. He shades his eyes against the sun and raises one hand, but he doesn't smile. I look at my bucket. I look at Otto and he nods towards the ladder resting against the roof. 'What are you waiting for?' he growls.

With a sinking heart, I climb up the ladder and sit on the sloping roof. Leo is opposite me. I know he's looking at me, but I ignore him and plunge the sponge in the bucket and start to aggressively scrub the roof. Why does pigeon poo need to be cleaned off a roof anyway?

After a few minutes of awkward poo clearance, Leo clears his throat. 'Kat, I need to talk to you,' he says quietly. Otto is just a few metres away, rearranging his kayaks.

'Well, I don't want to talk to you,' I say.

'No. I had noticed. You keep running away. I don't know what you heard the other night –'

'I heard *everything*,' I say, finally looking up at him.

'I just need to say one thing.'

I drop the sponge in the bucket. 'Go on, then. What's the one thing you want to say?'

'I didn't know Peeta was going to turn up like that and I didn't know you were standing behind me when I said . . .' He drops his voice. Otto is somewhere below us banging kayaks around and whistling.

'Have you forgotten what you said?' I ask. Now it's Leo who is looking away. 'How being with me meant nothing to you?'

'No.' He shakes his head.

'So is that it? Have you said your *one thing*?'

He sighs. 'It's complicated, Kat.'

'No. It's *simple*. You spent five days with me, on our own, and never once mentioned that you had a girl-friend.' My heart is pounding and nothing can stop the words from pouring out of me. 'You know what? Who cares? I'm not that disappointed, Leo.' Now I'm lying, I can't stop. I enjoy seeing the confusion on his face. 'It didn't mean much to me either. We've got nothing in common. We just spent a few boring days together so forget about it . . . I have.'

'That's what you think?' His face looks dark, cold.

For a moment, I don't speak. He looks so different from the boy I held hands with on Vilda. 'Yes. That's *exactly* what I think,' I say. Neither of us are bothering to keep our voices down now and I notice that Otto has stopped whistling.

'OK. I won't bore you for another minute.'

'Good!' I shout, and then I do something that seems like a brilliant idea for about two seconds: I throw my bucket of dirty water at him.

The bucket empties over Leo, the roof and me, then crashes to the ground.

He stares down at his soaked T-shirt, and then, without looking at me, throws his own bucket to the ground, jumps off the roof and walks away into the woods. Otto watches him go, then looks up at me, his face baffled . . . and a bit wet.

Suddenly, all the pleasure I got from saying those things to Leo and throwing the bucket at him vanishes and the ache comes back, only this time it's worse than ever. I need to be back in my attic room, right now. I scramble down the ladder. Otto is inspecting his bucket. 'Sorry,' I mutter, but that's all I can say without crying. Then I grab my paper bag from where I dropped it and run into the woods, making sure I go in the opposite direction to Leo.

I breathe deeply, trying to control the tears that are threatening to spill over at any moment. Today is Wednesday. Tonight I will go to the dock and one of my friends will be on the boat and then everything will be OK . . . everything will be *OK*. I tell myself this again and again, then I rip open the paper bag. Being sad makes me extremely hungry.

I pull out a squashed bun – Leo trod on my cinnamon bun!

Now nothing can stop the tears.

When I get in, I let myself get very low. First, I lie flat on my face on my mattress. I do this for an hour. Next I try to cheer myself up by reading *Grazia*, but handbags and colour-pop coats seem to have lost their magic. I drop the magazine in the recycling. Frida can use it to light the stove.

A run with Nanna eventually picks me up and when I go to the dock to wait for the last boat from Stockholm, I'm actually smiling at strangers. I watch passengers pour off the boat and drift into the forest. Eventually, the boat is empty and it's just me left on the jetty. My smile disappears. Deep down, I suppose I knew my friends wouldn't be allowed to come here, but that didn't stop me from imagining how amazing it would be to see one of them standing on the boat, jumping up and down and calling out my name.

I walk slowly back to the cabin, going the long way along the path that hugs the edge of the island. The sea is washed pink by the evening light and totally still. I go past Reception Rock and even though I've not got my phone I suddenly want to swim out to it. When I sit on that rock, I feel closer to my friends and home. I kick off my sandals and pull my dress over my head. I'm always wearing my bikini these days.

I tread over the rocks and slip into the glowing sea. After a few strokes, I dive down and my whole body is wrapped in cool, silky water. The shock feels good. I roll over and float on my back, kicking myself further out to sea and towards the rock and letting the last of the evening sun warm my face.

Soon, I'm climbing up on to the rock, then I sit hugging my knees and stare at the horizon. The more I try to find the exact point where the sea meets the sky, the further away it seems to get. A splash makes me look up. I see a figure in a kayak coming towards me. For a second, my heart speeds up and I actually consider jumping into the sea, but then I see that the figure is wearing a polyester tracksuit and a blue cap: Otto.

'*Hej*,' he says, raising a hand. He draws alongside me.

'*Hej*.'

'Mind if I join you?' I shrug. I'm not really in the mood to chat, but I don't own the rock. 'Sit on this,' he instructs, passing me one end of his paddle.

'What?'

'Sit on it.' I frown, but do as he says. He holds his end of the paddle across his lap so that he's anchored in place. 'Now I won't drift off,' he says. It's like we're sitting next to each other, only I'm on a rock and he's in his kayak. He takes a roll-up cigarette from his top pocket and lights it by striking a match against the side of the kayak. Next, he pulls a can of beer out from somewhere around his feet and opens the tab with a hiss. He takes a sip of beer. '*Skål!*' he says, toasting the sunset.

I laugh. 'I thought you were supposed to be a fitness freak?'

'Nobody's perfect,' he says with a shrug.

'You can say that again.'

Together we watch the sun slowly sink towards the pale horizon. 'You ran well today.'

'No I didn't. I was so slow. I think I'm actually getting worse at running.'

He shakes his head. 'You didn't pace yourself,' he says, jabbing his beer can in the air to emphasise his

181

point. 'You were too fast at the start.' I sigh and start to pick at the dry green plant that grows on the rock, crumbling it between my fingers. 'You know, Kat, we have a saying here in Sweden: *Alla är vi barn i början.*'

'I assume you are going to tell me what it means.' I know I sound sulky, but I don't want a language lesson.

'It means: *We all start out as children* . . . It means that beginners make mistakes.' I lean forward and trail my fingers in the sea. Suddenly, Otto changes the subject. 'Did you know that I've known Leo since he was born?' I narrow my eyes. What's Otto up to? 'He was a happy little boy and as soon as he could talk he would make me take him out on my boat. We used to visit the little islands and he collected, you know, *sniglar.*' He wiggles his finger round in the air, drawing a spiral.

'Snails?'

'Yes, snails! Can you believe it? He kept them alive and gave them names.'

A few days ago, I would have loved to hear this story, but right now, I can't stand it. 'I think I might swim back,' I say.

Otto acts like I haven't even spoken. 'He was very happy . . . but people have to grow up, become more serious. The other day, though, Leo's face was shining like he was six again and he'd just found the best, rarest snail in the world.'

I'm starting to lose track of Otto's story. I stand up, releasing his paddle. 'I really think I should be getting back,' I say. I know he's trying to help out Leo, but it's not working. The image of a cute snail-collecting Leo doesn't cancel out the image of Leo with a secret girl-friend. I start to clamber off the rock into the sea.

'It was the day he brought back one of my kayaks – a double one – and I asked him what he'd been up to . . .' I drift away from the rock, but I'm listening. 'He told me that he'd just spent the day on Vilda with you. That's all he said, but he couldn't hide his smile. It was good to see him that happy again.'

I start to swim away. I think I've just been compared to a rare snail! For a minute, Otto's story makes me forget about what happened at the disco, and I just remember being on Vilda with Leo, when we were the only people on the island. 'Your legs are wonky!' Otto shouts. 'You need to sort that out before Tuff Troll.'

'Maybe I like swimming with wonky legs!' I call back, then I turn over and carry on with my breast-stroke, deliberately kicking my legs out at a weird angle. Otto's chuckles echo across the water to me and I realise I'm smiling too.

Tomorrow I'm going back to the dock, and the day after that, and the day after that! Right now, one of my friends could be packing her bags, getting ready to join me here on Stråla. The thought of this makes me swim on with renewed energy and I even sort out my wonky legs.

'That's my girl!' Otto shouts. 'Don't give up, and remember, *alla är vi barn i början!*'

FOURTEEN

'So, in your life,' Nanna says, 'you've kissed *three* boys.'

'Technically,' I say. We're on one of our daily runs, heading towards Otto's hut. I suppose it's pointless training with Nanna: I've been to watch the ferry come for the past three days, but I'm always left standing on the dock alone. Each time the boat leaves, I feel a bit more disappointed because the more I train with Nanna, the more I want to enter Tuff Troll. My body feels strong and when I run I can control my breathing. Even my heart has stopped racing uncontrollably, but I can't enter the race without one of my friends. I've tried ringing them, but even though I've sat for hours on Reception Rock, I haven't had a single bar of reception . . . I am, however, getting an incredible tan.

'Technically? What do you mean?'

'Well, there was Tom Lord in Year Seven. It was in an English lesson in front of the whole class. We were acting out Romeo and Juliet and I was supposed to be dead. Miss told him to kiss my hand, but instead he went for my mouth and he *lingered* there. He got three Bad News stickers for kissing me.'

'What about number two?'

We run past Otto, who's standing by the path with a stopwatch. 'Hopeless!' he yells. 'Try and do the next lap in under twenty.' We run on, apparently ignoring him, but I notice both of us speed up.

'Number two was with Kyron at the end of the Year Nine Hallowe'en disco.'

'Better than the dead kiss?'

'Not really. I had vampire teeth on and he was wearing a Morphsuit. I'm not sure if it counts as a kiss if there's a layer of fabric between your lips. Plus, I didn't realise we were kissing. I was pretending to bite his neck for a selfie and he got the wrong idea.'

'Number three?'

I tell her about Joel in the wardrobe. It takes an entire lap of the island, but I do go into a lot of detail. 'They don't sound like very good kisses,' she says. 'In fact, I'm not sure they even count as kisses.'

'Maybe they were no good because I wasn't the one doing the kissing.'

'Right. Next time you find yourself in a kissing situation, make sure you're in charge,' says Nanna. 'OK. Time to Fun Run. You copy me.' She runs along the path swinging her arms round and round like a windmill. Nanna's very distracting – like a talking Labrador puppy. Sometimes she even makes me forget about Leo. I follow her, my arms flying round. Nanna invented Fun Run on our second day of running together. Basically, we take it in turns to do stupid things and the other person has to copy. No excuses. I was reluctant at first, but it is very fun.

'Come on,' says Nanna. 'It's your turn. My arms are about to fall off.'

'I choose . . . Creeping Elf!' We both make ourselves as small as possible as we run and hold our hands in a sneaky way. No way would I ever do this at home. Nanna's really good at it. She shoots ahead of me into the *mötesplats* and I follow her. I'm just about to yell 'Wait for me!' in the Creeping Elf voice when I see Leo and Peeta step out of the shop. Immediately, I straighten up and lose the sneaky hands. Standing tall, I run straight ahead, wishing my shorts were a bit less flappy . . . and didn't gape quite so much at the crotch.

'*Hej!*' says Nanna, running over to them. Sometimes she can be a bit too friendly.

'Remember we're being timed,' I say, but she ignores me and starts chatting away with Peeta. I join them and hover on the edge of the circle, studying the plastic bear, the boxes of vegetables and my nails – wow – they look *so* bad. As Peeta's explaining, in detail, why her trainers have such good arch support, I finally allow myself one tiny, fleeting glance at Leo. He's standing there, arms folded, staring at the ground, looking as uncomfortable as me.

'Hey, Kat,' says Peeta suddenly. 'Has your friend arrived yet?'

'Not yet,' I say. I know this is the moment when I should admit that there is no friend coming to Stråla, that there never has been, but Peeta rests her hand on Leo's back and this is enough to make me say, 'But she'll be here soon.'

'Great! I can't wait to meet her.'

'Come on, Nanna,' I say, tugging her away. 'Otto's waiting for us.'

As we run into the woods, Nanna calls back to them, 'See you at the disco tonight?' The disco. After what happened last week, I'm not sure I can face it. 'You are coming, aren't you?' she asks. 'Promise you'll come.' She looks up at me with her puppy face, her eyes big and hopeful.

'OK,' I say. 'I'll come.'

*

That evening, after I've done my make-up and spent an hour trying on all the clothes in my suitcase then dropping them on the floor because they look too 'resplendent', I sit on the steps outside the cabin and let my hair dry in the sun. Frida's gone to Nils's for dinner and I'm on my own. Music floats from the other side of the island. Is that 'Guantanamera'? Otto loves that track. Nanna will be wondering where I am.

I look down at my sundress and sandals, at my little blue bag. I don't want to go. I know I said that I wouldn't let Leo or Peeta stop me from doing anything, but I can't watch Peeta running her fingers through Leo's hair and resting against him . . . or Leo looking everywhere but at me.

Somewhere in the distance, a horn blasts: the last boat from Stockholm. Why did I ever think one of my friends would be allowed to come out here, all on their own? Britta always says I'm 'naively optimistic', and she says it in a really annoying voice, like she's my mum and I'm five . . . But what if one of my friends *is* on the boat? What if one of them is about to be dumped on this island in the middle of nowhere and is expecting me to be there, waiting for them?

Naively, I jump to my feet. Then I dash into the cabin and grab my trainers (optimistically).

If I run, I can get to the dock in time!

I burst out of the woods just as the boat is coming to a stop. The steward jumps down and starts securing the gangplank. I scan the deck. A crowd of children wearing identical yellow T-shirts are leaning over the railing, yelling at each other. The low sun is shining into my eyes, but I can just about make out a dark figure, a girl, standing slightly apart from the others. I shade my eyes. She's wearing black laddered tights, tiny denim cut-offs, scuffed boots and a loose white shirt. She has messy black hair and two thick silver chains hang round her neck.

'Pearl?' I whisper, amazed. My 'pretty fit' friend – who shoplifts, lies, and swears – has come all the way to Stråla! I stare, checking it's actually her. She looks like a crow in a field of sunflowers. She lifts one hand, tucks in her thumb and wiggles her fingers, lazily. It's our Ladybird wave, the wave she invented when we were five. Somehow, she's managing to do it sarcastically. Mouth hanging open, I wiggle my fingers back. *Pearl.* Here? On Stråla?

She sticks a cigarette into her mouth and heaves a huge sports bag on to her shoulder. As the children crowd to get off the boat, she pushes a path through them, her bag knocking into their heads. Then she stomps down the gangplank, walks up to me and drops her bag at my feet. Lighting the cigarette, she takes in the towering pine trees, the glowing rocks and sparkling sea. 'God,' she says, sucking on the cigarette, 'what a dump.' She blows smoke out of the corner of her mouth. 'What are *you* staring at?'

'You,' I say, shaking my head and smiling. 'You *actually* came.'

'Yeah, well. Free holiday. Carry that, will you?' She nods at her bag. 'I've been dragging it all over

Stockholm,' – she strides along the path that leads into the woods – 'the most boring city in the world.'

'Wait for me!' I call out, picking up her bag. I run after her as she disappears into the shadows of the trees. Whatever happens, I can't let Pearl out of my sight for a second.

She quickly fills me in on all the gossip from home. 'Jake's got a tattoo of a panda on his back because, apparently, he loves pandas. It looks like something you'd draw, and it's got *four* eyes. I've been banned from Superdrug because I had a fight with Amber by the nappies . . . with nappies. They said we made a baby cry . . . which is a *lie*. The baby *loved* it.' She pauses to flick her cigarette butt on the floor and I rush to pick it up. 'And I saw Bea Hogg *dancing* in town, tragic, and your freak-friend Betty is going round wearing a beard. Oh, and Tiann's going out with Levi. I just hope she doesn't forget about Oy.'

'Who's Oy?'

She stops and looks at me like I'm an idiot. '*Oyster*. My fish. He's a clownfish. You know, a Nemo.'

'You've got a clownfish?'

'Yeah.' She scowls. 'So what?'

'Nothing. I've just never heard –'

Suddenly, she puts her finger against my lips. 'Shut up,' she says, tilting her head to one side. 'Can I hear . . . *ABBA*?' Her eyes light up and she almost smiles. 'I can. Someone's playing ABBA!'

'It's from the disco. I didn't know you liked ABBA.' Recently, Pearl stopped listening to R&B and got heavily into hip-hop and grime. That's when she started wearing lots of leather and metal. ABBA really don't go with her studded wristbands.

'*Everyone* likes ABBA, Kat.' She walks towards the music.

'But we're right by the cabin. Let's get some food and unpack your stuff. Say hello to Frida.'

'My bag will be alright here and your auntie can wait.' She takes the bag off me and drops it behind a rock. 'Anyway, I want chips. C'mon.'

'But Peeta will be there,' I say desperately, 'and Leo.'

'So?' She starts to walk on. 'What happened when Leo's girlfriend turned up? Did she punch you for playing around with her man?' She drops her head back and laughs at the idea.

I catch up with her. 'I wasn't playing around with him. We just . . . went swimming and talked.' I can't tell Pearl how I felt when I was with Leo, or what I imagined might happen. Instead, as we walk along, I describe the conversation I overheard. 'Peeta said I was "*blåst*" – she was basically saying I'm an airhead – and Leo just sat there agreeing with her.'

'Ouch. What did you do?'

'I marched up to them –'

'And decked Leo?'

'No! I told him I was entering Tuff Troll with one of my friends.'

She laughs and shakes her head. 'So what does he look like, this Leo?'

I think about his curving mouth and his dark eyes that seemed to see everything. I shrug. 'Nothing special.'

Pearl is watching me out of the corner of her eye. 'Clearly Peeta's a cow and Leo's a player,' she says. 'They both need to be taught a lesson.'

'Oh my God. No they *don't*, Pearl.' I grab hold of her arm. 'This is a small island. I don't want any trouble. And I don't care about them. I just want to forget about Leo and take part in this race. It will be awesome. Imagine telling everyone back at school that we swam across the sea to an island.'

'They won't believe it,' she says.

'Exactly. So forget about Leo and Peeta, this is about Kat and Pearl!'

She grins and her eyes flash. 'Yeah, totally . . . But I'm still going to get them.' Then she shakes me off and strides towards the *mötesplats*, singing along to 'Mamma Mia' and taking swipes at the branches that get in her way.

When we get to the cafe, Pearl looks around with narrowed eyes, taking in the wooden benches, the fairy lights and the spectacular sea view. A lot of customers stare at her too – she looks so out of place – but she doesn't care. If anything, she stands a little bit taller, raises her chin fractionally. She likes being looked at. The sun has begun to melt into the sea and even Pearl is glowing a pretty pink colour. It's good to be by her side.

Nanna waves at us from our rock in the corner. She appears to be playing chess with a milkshake. 'Who is *that*?' Pearl asks.

'My friend, Nanna.'

'*Nanna?*' She laughs.

'Yeah, remember you're called Pearl.'

'*Nanna!*'

'You'd better be nice to her,' say. 'She's my only friend on the island.'

'She makes Betty Plum look normal.'

'Pearl.'

'OK. I'll be nice . . . to the freak.' She glances at the blackboard menu. 'Get me some chips, will you? And

I want one of those.' She points at a green cocktail that's being carried past on a tray.

'They won't let you have it,' I say. 'You're underage.'

'Kat, this is *Europe*. You can drink wine when you're, like, ten.'

'Not in Sweden.'

'Then I'll buy some vodka from the shop.'

'You can only buy low alcohol beer in shops. To get alcohol you have to go to a state-run off-licence.'

'Which is . . . ?'

'In Stockholm.'

'*What*? It's Friday night, Kat!' I shrug. She stares at me for a moment then rolls her eyes. 'Alright. I'll have an apple juice . . . *please.*'

We weave through the crowded tables with our drinks. We know where we're going: Nanna is jumping up and down and shouting, 'Over here! Over here!' We sit down and Pearl leans back against a convenient rock.

'This is Pearl,' I say. 'My friend from home.' I've told Nanna all about Pearl on our runs around the island.

'Pearl . . .' Nanna's eyes are wide, like she's meeting a film star. 'You look amazeballs!' Pearl slowly sucks her drink through a straw. '*Just* like . . .' Nanna pauses dramatically. 'Jack Sparrow!'

Pearl stops sucking. 'Are you saying I look like Johnny Depp? The pirate?'

'Yes!' Nanna grins.

Pearl stares hard at Nanna. Every muscle in my body tenses, but Nanna just sits there smiling sweetly, like a kitten trying to make friends with a tiger. 'A pirate,' Pearl says. 'Yeah, I like that. By the way.' She points her straw at Nanna's T-shirt. '*That*, I love.'

Nanna looks down. She's wearing a T-shirt that says 'I Pooped Today!' with a happy-looking stick man punching the air. I'm fairly certain Pearl does not love the T-shirt. I'd say she hates it.

'You can have it.' Nanna pulls the T-shirt over her head, carefully folds it and passes it to Pearl. Thankfully, she's wearing a vest underneath. A vest that has a six pack printed on it.

Pearl holds the T-shirt and stares at Nanna, amazed. 'Cheers,' she says uncertainly, and then she smiles. It's over very quickly, but it was definitely a smile.

Leo and Peeta don't come to the disco. All evening, I look out for them, dreading the moment that they turn up, but they never show. My mind keeps torturing me with images of them alone together at Leo's tent, watching the sunset and eating Plopp. After Nanna has tried and failed to teach Pearl to play chess (Pearl throws Nanna's queen into the sea), we've danced to ABBA and Pearl has stolen an ashtray, I take her back to the cabin to meet Frida.

'*Hej*,' says Frida as I open the door. She doesn't look up from the book she's reading.

'Look who's here,' I say, trying to sound as cheerful as possible. Frida peers over the top of her reading specs and I push Pearl forward. 'This is Pearl.'

It's fair to say that Pearl doesn't always make a good first impression on adults. She scowls at Frida through her messy hair. 'Alright,' she says. Then, nervously, she reaches into her bag, pulls out a cigarette and shoves it in her mouth. Immediately, she takes it out and fiddles with it. Shreds of tobacco fall to the floor.

Frida puts down her book and gets to her feet. She opens her arms wide. 'Welcome, Pearl,' she says, then she wraps Pearl in an enormous hug. Pearl stands stiff and rigid, but this doesn't put Frida off. That hug goes on and on. If anything, Pearl's total stiffness encourages Frida to put more and more into the hug.

Eventually, Frida steps back and looks at Pearl, head tilted to one side. 'Your name suits you,' she says. 'Would you like some miso soup?' Pearl shudders and shakes her head. 'OK. Well, I'm going to listen to the sea.' She grabs a jumper off the back of a chair and drifts out of the cabin.

Pearl stares after her. 'She is . . .'

'Weird?' I suggest. To Pearl, ninety-nine per cent of the human race is weird.

'Yeah. Now, where am I sleeping?'

★

She is not impressed with the sleeping arrangements.

'I'm sleeping in *that*,' – she kicks the mattress with her toe – 'with *you*?'

'You can pick your side.'

'That one,' she says, nodding at the half of the mattress not squished under the eaves. 'God, it's small up here and so hot.' She looks at me with wild eyes. 'Just being up here makes me want to hit something!' To avoid being hit, I let her smoke a cigarette leaning out of the attic window. This calms her down and then she starts to construct a wall along the middle of the mattress using my clothes and underwear.

'Pass me that vest,' she says. She tucks it in a gap then sits back to check out her work. 'Nice.' She nods her head. 'Right. I'm tired. Let's go to bed. I didn't go home last night and I only slept for an hour on the plane.'

'What?' I crawl into my side of the bed, taking care not to knock down Pearl's wall of pants.

She turns off the light, flops back on her pillow and puts her arms behind her head. She stares out of the window. 'My brother locked me out, again, so I just wandered around until morning when Mum got back from her boyfriend's house. I hate him. He's an idiot.'

'Your mum's boyfriend.'

'No, Alfie. But I do hate Mum's boyfriend.'

'Did your mum mind you coming here?'

'Nah,' she says, sitting up to open the window. 'She's just happy I'm not at home fighting with Alfie. She said I could stay as long as I liked.' Pearl rummages in her bag. 'I need to text Tiann and find out if Oy is OK.' I watch as she turns on her phone, but I don't say anything. 'No reception,' she says. She sticks her phone out of the window. 'Nothing. Where can I get reception?'

'Oh, there is a place . . . I'll take you there tomorrow.'

'Sweet. Alright.' She settles back on her pillows. 'Goodnight, loser.'

'Goodnight, Pearl.' Suddenly, she sits bolt upright. 'What now?' I ask.

'Those stars are too bright!'

I roll over as she drapes one of my dresses across the window to make a curtain. 'You're the only person I know who doesn't like stars,' I say.

'Shut up, star-lover,' she mumbles. And those are the last words she says to me before she falls asleep.

I lie in the stuffy attic room, Pearl snoring quietly next to me. Even though the room's not big enough for two, and there's a good chance Pearl will upset every single person on Stråla, I'm still happy she's here. She makes me feel stronger. I glance over the wall of vests. Pearl is sprawled across the mattress, arms flung above her head.

Even when she's asleep, she looks like she wants a fight.

FIFTEEN

'Beautiful!' Pearl says. We're sitting on the beach looking at Reception Rock and it's another perfect summer's day. The sea is emerald green, the colour lightening towards the horizon, and the sun is warm on our shoulders. Pearl sucks on her cigarette and sighs happily. 'Gorgeous,' she says. It's her first cigarette of the day and she's enjoying it. It's also the last one in her pack.

After we've swum to the rock, we're going to the shop to buy her cigarettes. You have to be eighteen to buy them in Sweden, but she's confident this won't be a problem. This is one shopping trip I am not looking forward to. As Pearl smokes the cigarette, her jittery body calms down. 'Are you sure about this?' I ask. Pearl insists that she can swim out to the rock and that she's 'a freakin' amazing swimmer'.

'Check out these guns,' she says, flexing her muscles.

'Where did they come from?' I ask. They are quite impressive.

'Me and Tiann have been going to the gym. Levi always lets us in for free.' She shakes her head. 'More Sellotape,' she demands. I add another strip to her phone nest. 'Right. Let's go.' She stubs out her cigarette and eases herself into the sea. 'C'mon.'

And that's how I find myself swimming in the Baltic with Pearl. I wouldn't say she's freakin' amazing, but I'm not worried about her drowning. She has absolutely no technique, but she's strong and soon we're hauling ourselves on to Reception Rock and Pearl is swearing about all the poo that's stuck to her knees. Sitting side by side, we turn on our phones. 'This had better work,' she says, 'or I'm going home.'

'You can always write a letter to Tiann.'

'By then Oy would be dead.'

She frowns at her screen. Nothing. I've got no reception either. *Come on, rock,* I think. *Work your magic.*

'So why's Oy such a special fish?'

Pearl sighs. 'I've already told you. He's a *clown*fish.'

'You could buy another.'

'He's not a goldfish, Kat. Clownfish live in a salt-water aquarium. Mine is a hundred and thirty litres.' I look at her blankly. 'It's huge. And it's full of living coral and I have tangs, dottybacks, dwarf angels.' As Pearl describes her tank, she loses her scowl and she starts waving her hands around. 'Oy is the best thing in that tank.'

'Is he the most expensive?'

'That's not it.' She kicks her feet in the water. 'I wish I had a fag,' she mutters. 'It's just that one of Mum's old boyfriends, Jon, gave me the tank.' She holds her phone over her head and waves it around. 'Anyway, the tank is in my room and the door's locked. Tiann has the key and is going to go round when Mum's at home to look after my fish. I'm paying her.'

I'm not that surprised Pearl hasn't told me about Oy or her other fish. Pearl has a lot of secrets. 'Why can't your mum or brother do it?'

'Mum would forget and Alfie would let them die. He'd probably poison them.'

We stare at our phones in silence. Suddenly, they start buzzing and vibrating. Two, then *three* bars of reception appear! Pearl screams, making a flock of seagulls take to the sky, and then we bend our heads over our phones and get to work. I've got twenty-six texts, but it's an email from Mum that I read first.

Hello Darling!

How are you? I hope you get this. Strála's the end of the world, isn't it?! I know you were a bit cross that we didn't tell you about Strála, but we thought it would be a nice surprise when you got to Sweden.

I miss you and Britta so much, but I'm sure you're having a wonderful time. Daddy says 'Hi' and wants me to pass on a big kiss to his little girl. We got your letter and are pleased you want to enter Tuff Troll. Dad's Googled it and says – taking into account your height, weight and previous experience – you might be able to complete the race in under ninety minutes, but he's worried that you will be the last one in. He doesn't want you to feel like you lost. Perhaps you should sit this one out? We're all entering the Cliff Hanger 12K in autumn, an endurance race in Dorset. Maybe if you start training now, you might be able to have a go at that?

Got to go. Bloomingdale's beckons! You should see the clothes I've bought. Don't worry, I'll share them with you.

Love Mummy

P.S. Write a letter to Britta. I think she might miss you.

209

I'm holding my phone tight in my hand. Mum has managed to annoy me from over a thousand miles away. I thought they'd be thrilled about the race. I even imagined her getting my message and proudly showing it to Dad, but I guess they shook their heads and tutted. They would never, *ever* tell Britta to 'sit this one out'. How many times has Dad said to Britta, 'Sweetheart, giving up is not an option.' Unless you are Kat. Then it's the only option.

I stare at my phone, not sure what to do next. Pearl's been involved in frenzied texting to Tiann and is relieved to discover that Oy's alive. She shows me several blurry photos of him. My reception flickers down to two bars. Quickly, I send a message to Britta: **Hey Titta, just wanted to let you know I'm alive. I hope you are looking after Pinky. If Mum rings, tell her I AM entering Tuff Troll. You could write to me if you like. x Kat**

'Who's Titta?' Pearl is reading over my shoulder.

'My sister. That's what I used to call her when I was little.'

'The one you hate?'

'I don't hate her.' This comes out loud. Pearl just raises one eyebrow and turns back to her phone.

I've had a lot of messages from Betty and Bea, both telling me that they aren't allowed to come to Sweden on their own, or even together. I text back, telling them the bizarre news that Pearl is sitting next to me right now. I include a photo to prove it. Pearl goes for her classic pose of a sneer and a single finger stuck up close to the camera.

'Reception's gone,' she says a few minutes later. 'Come on. Let's go. I want my fags.'

Pearl doesn't find swimming back so easy. In between wheezing and coughing she calls me names. I swim slowly next to her, but everything I say to encourage her just makes her madder. I look at the shore. It seems really far away and Pearl is very pale. Just when I'm wondering if I should get her to float so I can pull her in, a voice calls out, 'Stop splashing your arms around!' I turn round. Otto is paddling towards us on one of his kayaks.

'Oh, thank God,' Pearl says. 'Give us a lift, mate.' She starts to swim towards him.

'No, no,' he says, paddling backwards out of her reach. 'Don't quit. You're not a loser, are you?'

'Did you call me a loser?' Pearl does her hard face, the one that usually means serious trouble for someone, but today it just makes Otto laugh. Maybe it's the Sellotape harness, or it could be the flapping hands. 'Why don't you shut up?' she says. 'Because I am about to *drown* and it will be your fault!'

'Pain is temporary, young lady. Quitting lasts forever!'

'Ahhh!' she screams. '*Death* lasts forever too, *old man*!' But after a few seconds of staring at Otto and treading water, she growls then starts swimming towards the shore.

Otto paddles behind her, just out of her reach. I know this because when he says something particularly annoying, like, 'Losers quit when they're tired. Winners quit when they've won!' she takes a swipe at his kayak.

Eventually, she gets close enough to the beach to crawl in on her hands and knees. Then, before she's even clear of the water, she falls face down on the smooth rock, her legs still dangling in the sea. Otto watches as I try to pull her further up the rock by her hands. 'C'mon, Pearl,' I say. 'Get up.'

Eventually, she rolls on to her back. Then, groaning, she props herself up on her elbows. She pulls her phone out of the Sellotape. 'Jesus.' She tugs at the tape. 'How do I get this off my hair?' Looking up, she sees Otto in his kayak. They stare at each other. Pearl's shoulders are shaking. 'Go on,' she mutters. 'Say it.'

Otto narrows his eyes and Pearl narrows her eyes back. They are having a scowl-off. They're both good. I can't tell who is going to win. 'Say what?' he asks.

'You know,' she says. 'Winning's like a sandwich. Don't forget the bread, or some rubbish like that.'

'Failure is not falling down. It's refusing to get up.'

'Who said that?' she asks, grabbing my arm and pulling herself to her feet. 'A dumbass in a kayak?'

Otto laughs then paddles away. 'Good swim!' he calls over his shoulder.

'Dick,' says Pearl. But she says it quietly.

'So that's Otto,' I say, 'the guy who's going to help us train every day and the person who runs Tuff Troll. It's really great that you made such an effort to be charming.'

'I might kill him,' she says, as she starts to dry off, 'or *you* if you don't get me some fags *right now*.'

'I'm sorry,' says Juni, smiling at Pearl, 'but I can't sell you tobacco because you are under eighteen.'

'I'm not!' Pearl puts both hands on the counter. 'I'm *eighteen*. Tell her, Kat.'

'Er,' I say. Juni stares at me. 'It's true. Pearl is definitely eighteen.'

'Then why did your aunt give me this?' Juni points at a picture pinned behind the till. It's a very accurate drawing of Pearl, complete with leather wristbands, wild hair and angry face. Coming out of cartoon Pearl's mouth, in cheery bubble writing, are the words, '*Jag är femton!*'

Juni translates for Pearl, pointing at each word in turn. 'I. Am. Fifteen.'

'Give me that!' Pearl leans forward and tries to grab the picture.

'Oh no you don't,' says Juni, folding her arms and standing solidly in her way.

'Having that picture up there is abusing my rights!' Pearl's fists are clenched so tight that her knuckles have gone white.

Juni watches her for a moment, then says, 'You are not buying any cigarettes from this store. But I have just made some cinnamon buns. Would you like one?'

'Too expensive!' spits Pearl.

'It's a gift,' says Juni, taking one from the cake stand and putting it in a paper bag. 'They taste nicer than cigarettes.'

'I doubt it,' says Pearl. But after scowling at Juni for a moment, she snatches the bag and walks out of the shop.

'*Tack*, Juni!' I say, smiling as sweetly as possible.

I catch up with Pearl in the woods. She's peeling strips off the cinnamon bun and stuffing them in her mouth. 'I *hate* it here,' she says darkly.

'Do you want to go home?'

'Yes!' She marches on. 'No . . . not really. I hate it there too. I just really, really *need* a cigarette. Ahhh!' she screams, punches a tree, then has a massive bite of bun. I'm filled with dread when I imagine what the next few days will be like, with Pearl stomping round the cabin, swearing at me and Frida and craving nicotine. 'Stop looking so miserable,' snaps Pearl. 'Don't worry. I won't freak out . . . much.'

'Why don't we go for a run,' I say desperately. 'It might distract you from smoking.'

'Are you serious?'

'We have to run five kilometres in Tuff Troll.'

'Look, Kat, about this race –'

'Don't,' I say. '*Please* don't say you won't do it.'

'Why's it so important that we do the stupid race?'

'I have to enter because *no one* thinks I can do it,

Pearl.' I pull her back so we are facing each other. 'Leo thinks I'm a joke, so does Peeta. My mum and dad have told me to give up. Even Frida, *Miss Positivity*, thinks I shouldn't bother.'

Pearl makes her eyes go wide, like I'm mad. 'Calm down,' she says. 'Just forget about it and we can have a laugh.' She looks around at the trees and wrinkles her nose. 'We can sunbathe and stuff.'

'No we can't! Right now, I need *one* person to say, "Course you can do this, Kat." And that person is *you*!' I actually press my finger into her chest as I say this.

She looks down at my finger and then slowly back at me. I'm not sure what she's going to do, but at that moment we hear footsteps and look up and see Peeta running towards us. She's wearing tight black running leggings and special sunglasses with an elastic strip to stop them falling off. Her gold chain is bouncing on a tiny sports bra.

She stops in front of us and rests on her knees. 'Your friend has come,' she says, breathing heavily.

She can't hide the surprise in her voice. She straightens up and stares at Pearl, a dangerous thing to do at the best of times, but very risky when Pearl is nicotine deprived. 'So this is your "really fit" friend. The one who is going to help you win the race.' Then she does her smile, the one intended to make you feel small and pathetic.

Pearl understands that smile. She practically invented it. Popping the last bit of bun in her mouth, Pearl licks each finger in turn, never taking her eyes off Peeta.

'This is my friend from home,' I say, 'Pearl, and –'

'Are you Peeta?' Pearl interrupts.

'That's right.' As she talks, Peeta taps at some sort of monitor strapped to her arm. 'I just did my fastest kilometre!'

'Feeling tired?' says Pearl.

'A little. I have just run 10k.'

'Losers quit when they're tired.'

'I wouldn't know about that,' Peeta says with a laugh, 'because I *never* quit. Listen.' Her face softens.

'Are you guys sure you should enter Tuff Troll? It's a difficult race.'

'I don't know,' says Pearl, laughing. 'Unlike you and Kat, I'm not that bothered about it. I haven't even brought my trainers.'

Peeta smiles and raises one eyebrow. 'Challenges are for winners. *Excuses* are for losers. I'm doing another lap.' Then she brushes past us and carries on running along the path.

We watch her go. 'So are we entering Tuff Troll?' I ask.

Pearl looks at me through narrowed eyes. 'Looks like I'm going to have to. There's only one problem.'

'What?'

'I wasn't joking about the trainers. I haven't got any running stuff either. Hang on.' She looks down the track. 'Got to have the last word.' But Peeta's nowhere to be seen. 'That,' she says, punching another tree, 'is *so* annoying.'

★

Frida drops a plastic bag on the kitchen table. 'Help yourself,' she says to Pearl. 'I always bring my yoga gear, but I hardly ever use it. I'm sure it will be fine for running.' Pearl peers into the bag. Between her thumb and finger, she pulls out a pair of lime green harem pants. Daisies are embroidered round the hem. This is followed by an orange top covered in tassels. Pearl holds it at arm's length like it's contaminated.

'Tie-dye,' Pearl says. 'Did you do that yourself?' Frida smiles. 'You're very creative, aren't you? I liked the picture you drew of me. We just saw it at the shop.'

'And I like your lungs, sweetheart,' Frida says, giving Pearl a quick hug.

Pearl sighs deeply and steps away from her. 'Alright. I'll wear it.' She snatches up the clothes and climbs up to the attic to get changed.

Frida winks at me and tucks her towel under her arm. 'Enjoy your run!'

We sit on the veranda and soon Nanna turns up at the cabin with a pair of Sören's old trainers. Pearl has rolled up the sleeves of the top so the tassels are hidden and is wearing the trousers low on her hips. Her hair is tied in a big knotty bunch high on her head.

'Wow,' says Nanna when she sees her. 'Now you look like a pirate from a children's book!'

Pearl scowls and pulls on the trainers. 'These stink,' she mutters.

Nanna shrugs. 'That's because they belong to Sören.'

We head into the woods. 'Are we going to Fun Run?' asks Nanna, bouncing ahead of us up the path.

'What's that?' Pearl's hands dangle by her sides and she's barely lifting her feet off the ground. As we jog along the path, I explain the basic idea of Fun Run, with Nanna enthusiastically demonstrating each move.

'Don't forget the Freak Out,' she says, starting to scream and run like she's being chased by zombies.

'OK,' Pearl says, pausing to cough violently. 'Just so you both know, I am *never* doing that. Everyone stop!'

she shouts. 'Tired.' We walk for a few minutes until Pearl decides she's ready to run again. 'We do need something to make this better though,' says Pearl. 'Why do people do this? It's like torture. I think I might puke . . .' We all stop. 'Nope. False alarm.'

'It gets better,' I say. 'I like it now.'

'Well, you're weird. What we need is music.'

'Yes!' says Nanna. 'Like we're running to a disco.'

'Can't do it,' I say. 'My iPod battery ran out last week and I can't charge it.'

'Why not?' asks Nanna.

I laugh. 'Because there's no electricity.'

'We've got electricity at our cabin.' She says this like it's the most obvious thing in the world.

'What?' I stop running. 'Are you telling me that, all this time, you've had electricity?'

She nods. 'All the youth hostel cabins have electricity. They run off the same generator.'

'You never said.'

She shrugs and carries on running. 'You never asked.'

'I can have straight hair again,' I say, jogging after her, 'and take selfies . . . and play Toast Time!'

'More importantly,' says Pearl. 'We can have music. This afternoon I'm making us an awesome music mix for tomorrow's run. I'm going to give you two a *Fun* Run you'll never forget.' This idea obviously fills Pearl with energy. She whoops and picks up speed, which is lucky as we are just passing Otto's hut and he's on the prowl. Nanna grins and runs after Pearl.

'Don't clench those fists,' Otto shouts. 'Loosen those fingers!'

'What? Like this?' Pearl asks, and she sticks one finger up at him.

'Rude English girl!' he shouts and he starts to run after us. This makes Pearl and Nanna scream and run faster.

'Help!' shouts Pearl as we pass a couple of tourists. 'That old man is chasing us!'

'Fool!' he yells. I turn round. Otto has given up the chase and is staring at Pearl, arms folded. I'm about to say sorry – apologising for Pearl is something I'm good at – then I realise he's smiling.

'Lazy English idiot!' he shouts.

'Old Swedish perv!' she shouts, throwing her head back and laughing. Then she dashes off so fast I can barely keep up with her.

SIXTEEN

Otto must have forgiven Pearl because the following morning he turns up at our cabin with two printed training schedules. A printer! Suddenly, I'm seeing evidence of electricity everywhere.

'This is what you're going to do,' he says, handing me an A4 sheet. 'When you complete an activity, I tick it off.' He jabs at the little boxes running down the side of the sheet. 'Where's Pearl?'

'Down there,' I say, 'on the jetty.' She's been sitting there for the past two hours, in her bikini and pirate shirt, working on our running playlist. Spread around her are our three iPods and her laptop. Yesterday we had a big charging session over at Nanna's.

Otto goes over to her. 'Here we are, young lady.' He holds out her schedule.

Pearl pulls out one earphone, takes the sheet and drops it on the planks next to her. 'You shouldn't have bothered,' she says.

'Oh yes I should.' He stands over her, hands on his hips. 'I organise Tuff Troll and I'm responsible for all the competitors. You have got under two weeks to get fit. If I don't see you running round this island, swimming or kayaking *every single day*, you're not competing, and neither is your friend.'

'Alright, calm down,' she says, smiling under her long hair.

'After each session, you see me, and this afternoon, you are going out on one of my kayaks.' He stomps back to his moped and starts it up. 'Kayak hire is one hundred kronor an hour,' he shouts over the engine. Then he disappears in a burst of smoke.

The moment he's gone, Pearl picks up the sheet. 'Says here we should be running.'

'Two laps of the island.'

'Well?'

'Well, what?'

'Get your trainers on.' says Pearl. 'Time for a Fun Run!'

We meet Nanna outside the shop. She's just jogged a lap of the island and she's happy to do another one. I think she'd do anything Pearl suggested.

'Find the Fun Run playlist and put your earphones in,' says Pearl. We do as we're told, Nanna grinning with excitement. 'It's important that our music is synchronised or this won't work.'

'What won't work?' I ask. Pearl's air of mystery is starting to get annoying.

'You'll see. You just need to copy me.' She widens her eyes. She is so enjoying this. 'OK, press play on the count of three.' Obediently, Nanna's finger hovers over 'play'. 'One . . . two . . . THREE!'

We all press play and thudding hip-hop blasts into my ears. 'Keep it loud, but not so loud you can't hear me!' Pearl shouts. 'Enjoyin' the tunes?' Nanna nods eagerly. 'Ready to run?'

'Yes!' shouts Nanna.

'Ready for some *FUN*?'

'Yes!' Nanna's jumping up and down.

'Yes,' I say with a sigh, but neither of them hear me.

'Then let's do this!' Pearl takes the lead, running into the woods, one arm raised high, pumping in time to the music. Nanna follows her, her arm waving madly above her head and I jog after them. No way am I doing any air-punching. We've only been going for a minute or so when Pearl stops, spins round and starts to do a simple hip-hop move. 'Shoulder punch!' she shouts. 'C'mon, Kat, move those shoulders.'

'Really?' I say. I glance around to see if anyone is watching.

'Look at Nanna. She's got style! She's got the moves!' Nanna is shoulder punching like mental, her hair whirling round her face. It looks like I'm in one of those situations where you just have to join in. I start a half-hearted shoulder punch and Pearl nods her approval. 'C'mon, girls. Let's Fun Run!' And she's off.

Pearl's planned the whole route and every few minutes, she makes us stop and do another move. She's like a cross between a DJ and a dance instructor, and so enthusiastic I find it impossible not to start enjoying myself. We Harlem shake at the campsite (embarrassing), slide glide at the dock (painful) and twerk by the swings (inappropriate).

At one point we laugh so hard that Nanna has to sit on the floor so she doesn't wet herself. 'Come on,' says Pearl. 'Only one track left and I've saved the best till last.'

As we run into the *mötesplats*, I see Peeta coming out of the youth hostel. Leo isn't with her and I haven't seen him since he trod on my cinnamon bun.

'Copy me,' Pearl says, just as 'Super Trouper' starts to play. She drops to the ground. I think I know what's coming next, the most embarrassing dance move ever invented: the worm. Pearl starts to pop her body so she's wriggling forward in the dusty grass.

229

'Yeah!' says Nanna, throwing herself down next to Pearl and writhing around.

'Nice swag, Nan,' Pearl calls out. 'Kat. Get down here and crank your ass.' Out of the corner of my eye, I see Peeta gasp and put her hand up to her mouth, and that's when I get down and start to do the worm, enthusiastically, with passion and absolutely no swag. 'Go, Kat!' says Pearl. 'Move it, baby! Yeah! Just like a wiggly worm!' Pearl makes us worm to the entire song and by the end we've wriggled halfway across the *mötesplats*.

Pearl rolls on her back and shrieks with laughter. I pull out my earphones and lie next to her, every muscle in my body aching. I don't care what Peeta thinks because I've just been doing the worm with my friends and I feel so happy. Nanna sits up, dry grass stuck to her hair. 'Can we do it again?' she asks.

'No,' says Pearl, jumping to her feet. Out of her back pocket she pulls our training schedules. 'C'mon, Kat. We've got to see Otto.'

The three of us wander through the woods to Otto's cabin. 'Oi!' shouts Pearl. He's pulling kayaks out of a rack. 'We did it. Bet you thought we wouldn't.'

'Well done,' he says. He disappears into his hut. 'I saw you adding some core-strengthening exercises of your own invention. Good idea.' Pearl rests against a tree. Otto comes out holding a sheet of stickers. 'Which one would you like?' he asks, holding out the sheet.

For a moment, she just stares at the stickers. 'That one,' she says eventually. 'The purple sparkly one.'

Otto peels it off and sticks it over the first box. 'Good work, Pearl,' he says.

'Whatever.' She turns and walks away.

Otto comes over to me. 'Green, please,' I say.

'There we are.' He passes me my training schedule. 'By the way,' he says. 'You've got an unfinished job.' He nods in the direction of his hut. The roof is still covered in poo. 'Leo has taken off for a while, doing another job for me, so if you ever find yourself at a

231

loose end . . .' I look at him suspiciously, but he just shrugs and turns away.

'How come I don't get stickers?' asks Nanna.

Otto takes the biggest sticker – a round yellow cheese doing a thumbs-up sign – and sticks it on her forehead. 'Now you've got a sticker.'

SEVENTEEN

In theory, we follow Otto's schedule every day and we always have at least one Fun Run with Nanna. The quality of our training depends on Pearl's mood and how much she's craving a cigarette. Our training is often interrupted by sunbathing and eating ice creams, but I don't think Otto knows this and soon we've got a lot of stickers. Sometimes, I abandon Pearl and run off on my own. I love how invincible I feel – now I never get stitches or feel sick. I wonder if Stråla wasn't an island, just how far I could go. I'm starting to think it would be a very long way.

Because we've been living in our running clothes, getting ready for the disco on Friday is fun. I sit on the bed and talk to Pearl while she does her make-up and gets dressed. In complete defiance to the heatwave, she puts on black lurex leggings and a black top with a pair of red eyes glaring out from the front. Her hair is wilder than ever because she's decided not to bother washing it. She likes the way the sea makes it look 'freaky'.

'Do you know,' says Pearl as we walk into the cafe, 'you got ready in under *ten minutes*. That must be a record for you. You usually take ten minutes just applying lipstick.'

I shrug. 'I guess I've got out of the habit.' I look down at what I'm wearing: a white dress that looks so awesome against my tan that I don't care how resplendent it is. 'Do I look alright?'

'You look OK. Anyway, what's the point in dressing up? There are no fit boys here.' Pearl looks around the cafe while I rummage in my bag for my purse. 'Hang on,' she says. 'Who's *that*?'

I look up. Pearl is gazing at the stage where Otto's

disco is set up. Standing behind the decks is Leo. He's wearing a washed-out shirt with rolled-up sleeves, and his arms are golden from the sun. His hair is falling across his face. 'That,' I say, 'is Leo.'

'*That's* Leo? Huh.' She stares at him. 'I thought you said he was nothing special.'

'It's not just about looks –'

'His looks are sexy.'

'Stop looking, Pearl!' I try to pull her toward the cafe, but she refuses to move. In a way I can understand. All I want to do is stare at Leo. Together we watch as Peeta goes up to him and slips her arm round his waist. 'Let's get a drink,' I say.

'Why would he go out with *her*?' says Pearl.

'They're perfect for each other,' I say. 'C'mon, time for a Friday night fruit juice!'

'We'll see,' says Pearl, eyeing a half-empty beer bottle.

We find Nanna at our rock and, after a few minutes, Leo and Peeta come over and join us. It had to happen eventually. To begin with, it's massively awkward – Leo and I both spend a lot of time staring at the rock, or the sea, or anywhere but at each other, but soon Peeta and Nanna start talking about Tuff Troll, discussing the exciting news that Otto's actually got a prize for this year, an 'I ♥ Strála' hoodie.

Pearl is suspiciously quiet, following the conversation closely, but not joining in. Her eyes flick from person to person. Suddenly, she says, 'Hey, Leo.' He looks up. 'We've not properly met. I'm Pearl, Kat's friend.'

'Hello,' he says, frowning.

'She's told me all about you,' she says, smiling sweetly. She looks terrifying.

'She told me about you too,' he says. I did. In the few days we spent together, I told Leo everything about my life.

'Did she say that we're best mates? And that I always look out for my mates?' The smile has gone now and everyone is silent. I see Peeta move her fingers so they're resting against Leo's hand. I know exactly why she's done this.

Leo pulls away his hand and sits up. He looks Pearl in the eye. 'I think Kat can look after herself.'

'Yes, I can,' I say quickly. Pearl scowls at me, pulls out a packet of Lakrisal and throws two of the sweets in her mouth. A few days after Pearl was forced to stop smoking, she developed a new habit of eating Lakrisal – small salty liquorice lozenges – and now she averages three packets a day. 'So, what have you two been up to?' I ask with a smile. If I can get over Leo, then so can Pearl.

'Enjoying the island together,' says Peeta. I try to keep my smile fixed in place.

'And I've been doing a job for Otto,' says Leo. 'He arranges camping trips to different islands and I was checking the tents are OK. When I was out there, I went free diving.'

'What's that?' Pearl asks, her voice almost back to normal.

'You dive down into the sea using a snorkel and flippers, no oxygen tank.'

'It's pointless,' says Peeta. 'There's nothing to see around here.'

'I saw lots of things,' says Leo. 'Prawns and chequered snails, and perch and pike. It feels like another world. The colours are so vivid, even the seaweed looks beautiful.' As Leo talks he smiles, losing his frown. And even though I'm definitely over him, I realise I'm smiling too as he describes his dive. 'This perch had orange fins and was big. It swam right up to me and stuck its nose in my face . . . I actually felt it!' He laughs then trails off, aware that he's been talking perch for some time.

'They can grow up to a metre long,' says Pearl, ripping open a fresh packet of Lakrisal. 'They get big round here because of the herring.'

Suddenly, Peeta says, 'Do you like aquatic biology, Pearl?' It could be an innocent question, but not the way she says it. Clearly she's had enough of Leo and Pearl's cosy chat.

'What? Fish? Yeah. I love them. More than I like most people.' For a moment, they stare at each other. Then Pearl looks past her to the sea and her eyes go wide. 'Do you get whales round here?' she says, excited. 'I would *love* to see a whale.' For a moment, all her hardness slips away, and I see the girl I first met at nursery school. The girl who once cried when she found a squashed woodlouse in her plimsoll.

'I wish I could ride on the back of a whale,' says Nanna dreamily. 'It would be better than a dolphin, but my big dream is to ride *a manatee*.' There's a moment's silence, then everyone laughs, even Peeta.

'What's a manatee?' asks Pearl.

'Imagine a cross between a seal and a cow,' I say.

'And Otto,' adds Leo.

We start discussing which animals we'd most like to catch a ride with (me: extremely tame lion) and then Nanna announces that she's always wanted to kiss a platypus right on its bill and we move on to a whole new animal-based topic of conversation. Somehow, Nanna's habit of saying whatever pops into her head makes the awkwardness disappear, and we all talk at once.

Gradually, the sun slips below the horizon and Otto starts to play a mega mix of obscure Swedish dance-band tracks. I'm just explaining why kissing a slow loris would be a good experience when I notice that Pearl is shredding a beer mat – a warning sign that she badly needs a cigarette.

She groans and rolls her head back. 'I'm so bored I could eat a slow loris,' she says. 'I need to *do* something.'

'We could build a fire,' says Leo. 'I know just the right beach. Totally deserted.'

Perfect, I think.

'*Boring*,' says Pearl. 'What else?'

Leo shrugs. 'We could try the floating sauna. The hotel has a sauna on a raft in the sea – a really old-fashioned one with coals. No one goes there this late, because officially it's closed, but they never lock it and it should still be hot.'

'A floating sauna?' says Pearl, smiling. 'Now *that*, I like the sound of. C'mon, Kat.' She jumps to her feet. 'Let's get our bikinis. Time for my first ever sauna!'

Pearl and I take a shortcut to our cabin through the woods. The moment we're in the trees, she punches my arm. 'So, about Leo . . .' she says.

'What about him?'

'Nothing. Just –' She kicks at the pine needles and I smell the resin in the warm evening air.

'What?'

'I kind of think you might still *like* him?' She glances sideways at me.

'Well, I kind of think *you're wrong.*'

Pearl laughs. 'But you go quiet when he's around and you're always sneaking looks at him . . .'

'He *humiliated* me, Pearl.' I drop behind her, walking slower. I can't think about that night without thinking about what went before. 'Those five days I spent with him felt like the start of something.'

'The start of what?' She snaps a twig off a tree and starts breaking it into smaller pieces, dropping them on the path as she walks.

I can't tell her it felt like the start of *everything*; I don't think Pearl believes in love. 'It doesn't matter because then his girlfriend turned up and I found out what he really thought about me.'

'How do you know she's his girlfriend?'

I laugh. 'Peeta announced it the minute she arrived, just in case I hadn't got the message.'

'I don't know.' Ahead of me, Pearl shrugs. 'We've seen Peeta on her own loads. Tonight was the first time I've actually met Leo. They don't hold hands or kiss. They don't even talk that much.'

We walk on and fall into silence. I remember that night, how Peeta kissed him on the lips . . . but have I ever actually seen him touching her? I push the thought to the back of my mind. 'It doesn't matter,' I say. 'He still said those things about me.' Pearl's ahead of me, a silhouette on the moonlit path. I run to catch up with her. 'Anyway, who cares about Leo? I'm about to swim to a floating sauna with my bestie!'

'Yeah!' says Pearl and we link arms. 'Tiann is going to be so jealous.' Our feet crunch along the path. 'But can I say one more thing, you know, about Leo?'

I sigh. 'What?'

'Nothing really. It's just . . . he sneaks looks at you too, you know.'

We swim towards the sauna in a straggly line. Nanna and Pearl are at the front, whispering and giggling, followed by me and Peeta and then Leo. It's unusually dark tonight. The moon is a thin crescent of silver and the sea is black and feels spookily deep. Pearl turns round to check we're all keeping up. She looks at me and grins. She loves doing anything naughty, and breaking into the hotel's sauna is probably even better than underage drinking.

Soon, she's climbing the rusty ladder up to the platform and trying the sauna door. 'It's open,' she says, disappearing inside.

'Don't fall in the hole,' Leo calls after her.

We all shuffle into the sauna, feeling our way in the darkness. The platform wobbles from side to side. 'Is this made for five?' I say as I squeeze in, shutting the door behind me. Immediately, the heat hits my skin, drying my lips and throat.

'Watch it.' Nanna pulls me down on to the bench next to her.

'What?' My eyes adjust to the darkness and then I see a rectangular hole cut in the middle of the floor. Dark water is sloshing up through it. Leo and Peeta are sitting on the bench opposite me and Pearl is taking up a whole bench to herself. 'Is it safe to have a hole in the floor?' I ask, dipping my toes into the sea.

'Don't worry. This sauna's been here for years,' says Leo.

'Why's it got the hole?' I sit back and breathe out. The heat is starting to get to me, making me dizzy.

'It's well known that jumping into cold water

244

improves circulation,' says Peeta. 'Also, it's good for the immune system.'

'It just feels *lovely*,' says Nanna. 'It's a plunge pool. You get really hot, then jump in the hole and either swim out under the sauna, or climb back in for a bit more heat.'

'Cool. An escape hatch,' says Pearl. 'We are all going down there.'

'Can you hit your head on the platform?' I still don't like the look of it.

'Is you scared, Kit Kat?' Pearl leans over and strokes my hair.

'Yes, I am scared of jumping in that creepy dark hole full of fish, and lobsters, and *crabs* . . . But if you're all doing it, then so am I.'

'You'll be fine,' says Nanna. 'You just jump into the middle and start kicking straight away.'

Leo takes a ladle off a peg, scoops up some sea water and throws it on the coals. A burst of steam fills the cabin. 'This is freakin' boiling,' says Pearl. She laughs then starts to cough.

'Even the air tastes hot,' I say as sweat drips down my face. 'I don't get your obsession with temperature extremes.'

'We're tough like Vikings,' says Peeta. 'Maybe you can't handle it . . .'

'I can handle it,' says Pearl. 'It's *lush*.'

We sit it out for ten more sweaty minutes while Nanna and Leo swap tales of previous floating sauna visits. Peeta is strangely quiet. Usually she'd make sure we all knew she was the best at enduring heat, but she's just slumped against Leo, eyes down. Suddenly, Leo sits up and says, 'Who's jumping first?' We all stare at the black hole.

'Me!' says Peeta, standing up. She places her toes just over the edge, breathes deeply, raises her hands above her head and pauses to make sure we're all watching her. It looks like she's found her mojo again.

'Me actually,' says Pearl, and she gets off her bench and jumps straight into the hole, soaking Peeta and making Nanna collapse with laughter. Immediately, Peeta jumps in after Pearl, like she's going to get her.

'Oh my God,' says Nanna, as the platform rocks from side to side. 'They might have a fight!' She looks at me and then at Leo. 'Hang on. This is weird . . .'

'No it's not,' I say.

'Yes. *It is*. I'll leave you to it.' She gets up, holds her nose, and then jumps into the hole, barely creating a ripple. Suddenly, Leo and I are alone . . . in a very hot sauna.

We look at each other. The platform sways and the coals hiss. 'Shall I go next?' I say, breaking the silence. 'I don't want to be the last one.'

'No.' He stands up then immediately sits down. The sauna tips and water sloshes through the hole. He pushes his hands through his hair, glances at me, then looks away. 'I mean, don't go yet. I really do need to talk to you.'

For a moment, we sit opposite each other in the dark, shadowy cabin. It rolls gently from side to side. 'I've been thinking about how you must have felt, that night at the cafe, when Peeta turned up.' Just remembering the moment still makes my cheeks burn. I see Peeta slip her hands over Leo's eyes and then take her place next to him as if she belonged there. I stare at the water until Leo breaks the silence. 'You see, I was going to go to Stockholm the next day. I was going to tell Peeta not to come to Strála –'

'I don't want to hear about you and Peeta.' I stand up. The wooden boards feel cool under my feet.

'Please, listen,' he says. 'Peeta and I have been friends for a long time. Then, a few weeks before the summer holiday, we started going out.' I don't sit down, but I stand there, arms folded, and I force myself to listen. 'Peeta said she wanted to come here and compete in Tuff Troll and I said yes, even though I knew it was a mistake. When I kayaked to Strála, I had a lot of time to think. You see, right from the start, I thought we were better off as friends. That's really all I ever wanted us to be. Even before I met you, I knew we had to break up.' He looks at me. 'But when she arrived early, I didn't know what to do. She's had such a hard time recently, her mum and dad have split up and she's been really down. If she thought that you and me . . .' He takes a deep breath. 'It would have hurt her feelings so much.'

'So you decided to hurt me instead?' I feel the ache creeping back like it never went away. 'I guess I'm such an airhead you thought the words would just bounce off me! You said' – I point a finger at him – 'that being with me meant *nothing*.'

Now he's on his feet. 'I didn't know you were there, listening.'

'You still said it.' I say this quietly, but my heart is thumping wildly. 'Do you really want to know what I thought that night when Peeta arrived and when I heard you both laughing at me? I felt like my heart was going to break.' I don't care about hiding anything now. I want him to know the truth. 'Because, guess what, I *liked* you. So much. And the pathetic thing is,

I thought – for the first time in my life – that I had met someone who –' I pause, I don't know if I can say another word without crying – 'liked *me*.' I put my hand on my chest. 'But you can't have, can you? Because if you had, you would never have said those things.'

We stand facing each other. 'I got everything wrong,' I say, 'and now I want to forget about it, but most of all, I want to forget about *you*.' Every room should have a hole you can jump into when you're about to burst into tears. Without hesitating, I plunge into the black square of water.

I shoot down, water rushing into my nose and eyes. Wow! Icy, icy, icy! I go down, down, down, my lungs, toes and fingers stinging. Then I remember I'm supposed to be kicking and I force my tingling legs to move, pushing myself up through the black water towards the surface.

I burst out on the open water, and gasp, taking one huge breath after another until breathing stops hurting.

A thousand stars shine down on me, but the sea is as black and still. The only sound is my wild and frantic breathing. Over on the beach, I can see Pearl standing on a rock, looking for me. I wave and start swimming towards her.

EIGHTEEN

'Move those lazy butts!' Otto yells through the trees.

My legs feel like stone, but I force myself to run on.

'Stretch it out, Kat,' says Pearl. 'C'mon.' And she moves ahead of me. I can't let her beat me! We run up to Otto's cabin and Pearl screams with delight as she gets there just before me. I sink to the floor and rest against a tree, but Pearl jogs over to Otto and does something totally unexpected: *a high five*! Back home, Pearl would never ever allow her palm to slap enthusiastically against someone else's in a moment of triumph.

'Two kilometres in eleven minutes,' Otto says. 'Your fastest time yet, girls. But that's all you are doing today.

You need to rest so that you are ready for the race tomorrow.'

Since we swam to the sauna, Pearl and I have thrown ourselves into our training. Pearl claims she's motivated by getting a cigarette – Otto told her that when she gets forty stickers he'll give her one of his roll-ups – but I'm not so sure. Having seen the high five and the amount of time she spends here with Otto, eating liquorice ice creams and arguing, I think she might be motivated by trying to get his approval, definitely a first for Pearl.

I've thrown myself into training because now I want to do Tuff Troll more than anything. I don't even think it's got anything to do with Leo and Peeta any more. We've bumped into Leo a couple of times, and I let Pearl or Nanna do the talking. Leo and I have even stopped looking at each other. I still find not looking at Leo quite a challenge. I really should get a sticker for it.

'There you go, Kat.' Pearl drops my training sheet on my head. 'Thirty-eight stickers.' She kicks my foot.

'Get up. Nils is coming round to put beads in my hair and we have to carry this back.' I look up. Pearl is holding one end of a battered kayak. 'Otto says we can use it for Tuff Troll. We're allowed to pimp it.'

'What?'

'Paint it, write on it, whatever we like. He's scrapping it after the race.'

'Is it safe?' Wincing, I stand up.

Otto sticks his head out from his hut. 'Of course it's safe.'

'Then why are you getting rid of it?' I pick up my end of the kayak.

'Because it's really, really heavy.' Immediately, I drop the really, really heavy kayak on to the floor. He's not exaggerating. I take a deep breath and pick it up again.

'Bring it to *mötesplats* this afternoon,' calls Otto as we stagger into the woods. 'In the morning, I'm taking all the kayaks to Fejan, ready for the race in the afternoon.'

★

As we walk back to the cabin, we see something strange gathering in the sky: clouds, dark grey clouds, and we even hear some grumbles of thunder.

Then, as Nils is putting beads in Pearl's hair, it starts to rain. We all rush to the cabin door and watch as a summer's worth of rain plummets down. It's so heavy, it makes waves on the sea and the ground starts to steam. Pearl sticks her hand outside and fat drops splash her arm. 'It's warm!' she says.

Frida brushes past us and skips on to the beach in her pants and T-shirt. She puts her arms up to the sky and turns round and round. Nope. Cancel the pants. 'Let's go for a swim,' she calls.

'You're alright,' says Pearl, but Nils is keen. He runs after her, pulling his T-shirt over his head as he goes. 'Hey, Frida!' Pearl has to shout loud to be heard over the rain. 'Can we paint the kayak in the cabin?'

'Of course,' Frida says, before Nils pounces on her and they both tumble into the grey, choppy sea.

'C'mon,' says Pearl, thumping me on the arm. 'I know what we're going to do.'

We drag the kayak into the cabin and balance it on the table. Pearl hands me a brush. 'You add teeth here.' She points to the front of the kayak. 'And I'll do some skulls and stuff.'

'So it's going to be . . . ?'

'A pirate shark kayak.'

'Right,' I say, and I start to paint a row of white fangs.

'Make it grin,' says Pearl. 'I'm going to give it a name. What shall we call it?' She chews on the end of her paintbrush. '*Kick Ass? Epic Win?*'

'*Tragic Loss?*'

'What about: the *Pearly Queen?*'

'No way. I'm going to be sitting in there too.'

'I know,' she says, and she starts painting, the beads in her hair hitting against the side of the kayak. 'Teeth,' she reminds me. Obediently, I dip my brush in the paint and get back to work.

'What do you think?' Pearl asks, a few minutes later.

I look up. Written in sloping, dripping letters across the side of the kayak are the words: *Wild Kat*. 'Well? Do you like it?'

'What about you?'

She scowls. 'Do you like it, or not?'

'Yes,' I say, grinning. 'I love it.'

'Then shut up and finish those teeth. This is your race, Kat. I'm just coming along for the ride.'

When the rain clears up, we carry *Wild Kat* to the *mötesplats*. 'Everything feels different,' says Pearl as we walk through the woods, the kayak banging against trees, and, occasionally, a tourist.

'Muddy?' I ask, stepping round a puddle.

'I dunno,' she says. 'There are more people and the rain has made everything smell strange.' She sighs. 'I just can't believe Tuff Troll is tomorrow, and the next day we're going home. No more Lakrisal –'

'No more Nanna,' I say. 'No more Otto, *tampongs* or ABBA.'

'No more Sören dancing like a freak or seeing your auntie's butt first thing in the morning.' She trails off, kicking a branch off the path. It spins into the woods. She doesn't say the last 'no more', but it hangs in the air between us.

No more Leo, I think.

We find Otto setting up a marquee and bossing the islanders around, making sure every inch of the clearing is covered in Swedish flags. It's like Solsken, only it's nothing like Solsken. I'm wearing my spotty shorts, an old sweatshirt of Frida's and my feet are bare. When did I stop wearing shoes? Instead of make-up, I'm covered in paint, and my hair has been in the same plaits for three days.

'Girls!' Otto shouts, wobbling at the top of his ladder. 'Put your kayak with the others. Good God, what have you done to it?'

'Made it look bad ass,' says Pearl.

'Hmm.' Otto frowns. 'Have you both been resting?'

'Yes,' says Pearl, 'but I need one more sticker.' She gives the base of his ladder a kick.

He grabs a tree. 'When you finish Tuff Troll, when you cross the finish line, triumphant, *then* you get your last sticker.'

'And my fag?'

'I am a man of my word,' he says, thumping his chest.

'See you tomorrow afternoon, Otto,' I say. 'Any last advice?'

He frowns. 'Rub Vaseline on your thighs, crotch and armpits,' he says seriously. 'To stop the chafing.'

'Well, OK!' Pearl grins. 'We'll get a big tub right now.'

While Pearl stocks up on Lakrisal and other liquorice products that aren't available in the UK (because salty liquorice is gross), I find the Vaseline. At the counter, Juni hands me a letter. 'No glitter on this one,' she says. 'Much more sensible.'

I look at the handwriting and see faint pencil lines drawn under the address. There's probably only one teenager in the world who would do that: Britta.

Later, after we've done some packing and I've helped Frida wrap up the jewellery she's been making, I sit on the jetty and read Britta's letter.

Dear Kat

How are you? I've remembered to feed Pinky, but I think she must miss you because she's only bitten me twice since you've been gone. She's lost all her fiery passion. The house seems big and quiet and it's not the same without your pants and socks all over the landing, make-up spilt in the sink and the TV left on stand-by. I know you don't believe me, but I checked online, and leaving appliances on stand-by can add £76 to an annual energy bill!!!

What I'm trying to say is that I wish you hadn't gone away this summer and I'm looking forward to you coming home and adding £76 pounds to our energy bill.

I've told Mum and Dad to stop worrying about you entering this race. I reminded Mum that even though I'm the oldest, it's always you who's looked after me: you make me go to bed when I'm watching TV too late; when I failed my driving test, it was you who made me a 'Driving Sucks' cake - remember? And after I split up with Joel, you watched Mean Girls with me again and again. I tried to think of things I've done for you, but I didn't get very far.

I didn't even ask Mum and Dad to let you stay here this summer. Big mistake.

So, guess what? I've done something for you! I've registered you for Cliff Hanger. Please do it with me. Mum and Dad are always running off and leaving me on my own. It will be fab having someone to talk to.

Lots of love

Titta x

As I put the letter back in its envelope, Pearl sits down next to me. 'Your auntie says she's going round to Nils's place for "a quick sauna", which is clearly *not* what she's doing.' We watch the sun sink towards the horizon and soon the last slither of sunlight is melting into the sea, framed by an indigo sky. Pearl shuts one eye and holds up her hand, like she's squashing the last bit of sun between her thumb and finger. The sun gleams then vanishes below the horizon. She drops her hand. 'The last bit always goes too quickly.'

Pink clouds appear from nowhere. 'Now that,' I say, 'is a good sunset. Ten out of ten.'

'Suppose it's alright.' She starts to pick rotting wood off the jetty.

'How do you think we're going to do tomorrow?'

'We'll probably beat everyone and get the best time ever. They'll put up statues in our honour and *Wild Kat* will go on display at the cafe.'

'Or we might die,' I say. 'Look how far away it is, Pearl.' I point at Fejan. 'What was I thinking dragging you all the way out here just to help me prove I could do some ridiculously hard race?'

'Shut up, Kat. It's one kilometre away – we've swum further than that – and Otto said he'll have a support boat next to us all the way.' She flicks a bit of wood into the sea.

'We could drop out.'

'No way. I want my last sticker. Tomorrow we are taking part in Tuff Troll. It's happening, Kat. Accept it.' The violet clouds have become thin wisps. One by one, they fade away.

'And then . . .' I say.

She wriggles her toes in the water. 'Then we're going home.'

NINETEEN

'Kat, you idiot, you pricked me!'

At the last minute, Pearl has been struck with pre-race jitters. She's been fine all day, lounging on the jetty and eating cinnamon buns – apparently bulking up on carbs for the race – but since we arrived at the *mötesplats*, she's fallen apart. In the fast few minutes, she's sworn at Otto, hit me and called Nanna a freak. 'If Otto would let me be number seven, I'd feel fine,' she says. I'm pinning her race number to her back. We're numbers thirteen and fourteen. Obviously, I'm thirteen.

'There's already a number seven,' I say. 'Look. There he is.' An athletic Swede strides past us in a skintight triathlon suit. He looks like a superhero. All day, the ferry has been dropping off contestants and a crowd of spectators.

'Why are people staring at us?' asks Pearl, scowling at a girl who makes the mistake of glancing in our direction.

'It could be because we look so intimidating and sporty . . . Or maybe it's the massive Union Jacks you painted on our faces.'

'Yeah, well, we look awesome. They look like losers.'

I think they pretty much look like winners. All around us, fit blonde teenagers stretch out muscles, chat tactics and sip water. I'm worried, of course I am, but being brave for Pearl is helping me stay calm. Pearl rubs a bit more Vaseline under her arms. 'Talk me through it one more time,' she says.

'We run around Stråla, five kilometres.'

'Easy.'

'Exactly. Then we get in the sea and swim one kilometre to Fejan. You're wearing your costume?' Pearl twangs the strap under her vest. Everyone around us is dressed in high-performance fabric, but we're in our usual mix of spotty shorts, harem pants and tie-dye.

'And *Wild Kat* will be waiting for us there.' Pearl says. She knows it all really. We've been through it so many times. 'Then we kayak back to Stråla and win the race.'

'Ha!'

'Well, we win a sticker. Why are we doing this, Kat?'

I look around. Nanna and Sören are arguing over who gets to be number twenty and, over by the cafe, Peeta and Leo are having an intense conversation. 'I can't even remember now,' I say. 'But you wouldn't be here with me if we weren't entering Tuff Troll, and this summer's been amazing, hasn't it?' Pearl looks grim, but she nods. 'Dad says he races for the story. We're going to have a good story to tell when we get home.'

'*Ta era platser!*' shouts Otto.

'What's he saying?' Pearl grabs my arm as everyone goes towards the start line.

'Take your places.'

'Oh, God!'

Otto moves through the crowd, checking everyone is ready. He puts his hand on Pearl's shoulder. 'Find the zone,' he says. She nods. There is a flurry of last-minute stretching and bottles and T-shirts are dumped in a pile along with our tub of Vaseline. We find a place to stand in the middle of the group.

'Where's my zone?' Pearl hisses. 'I can't find it.'

I hold her hand. 'I'm your zone,' I tell her, hoping I sound much braver than I feel.

'Great,' she says sarcastically, but she squeezes my fingers.

Otto holds a horn above his head. 'On your mark.' He pauses and all around us teenagers drop down and crouch in athletic positions. 'Get set . . . Go!' He blasts the horn and we surge forward with the crowd.

'Go?' shouts Pearl as we jostle for space.

'Go. *Go!*' I yell, dropping her hand. We run into the woods, competitors streaming past us on all sides, pushing and shoving, and in minutes, Pearl and I are at the back. As we pass the campsite, Nanna glances over her shoulder, gives us an apologetic wave and then disappears round a corner. We run on alone.

'We knew we'd be left behind,' I say.

'I know. I just didn't realise it would happen so quickly,' says Pearl. 'Are we even going the right way?'

'Yes. We follow the purple arrows.'

The route is lined with spectators. A lot of them know us – both holidaymakers and islanders – and they call out our names and cheer us on. We have to run twice round the island then cut across the middle. It doesn't take long for the other contestants to lap us. First, Peeta and Leo run past, then Nanna and Sören. Nanna grins at us and does a bit of Creeping Elf and Windmilling to make us laugh, but when she sees Sören getting ahead she dashes off in her usual horsey style. Soon, we've done our laps and are back at the *mötesplats* and running to the guest harbour.

Otto's in his motor boat waiting for us. 'Get in the water, girls!' he calls through a loud hailer. 'I've got to check on the other swimmers, but I'll be right back.' The boat zooms off with a roar, bouncing over the surface of the sea. We pull off our clothes and trainers and chuck them to Frida.

'Energy gel,' says Frida, forcing us to drink a sachet of sugary gloop. Then we put on our goggles and run to the end of the jetty.

'Remember the story of the hare and the tortoise!' Nils calls as we climb into the sea.

'Great,' says Pearl. 'We're tortoises.'

'But if all the other competitors fall asleep,' I say, 'we stand a chance of winning.'

'Right,' she says. 'Now, shut up and swim.'

We plunge into the water and go straight into front crawl, keeping our faces down and breathing every three strokes, just like Otto taught us. We swim round the edge of Stråla, following the swimmers at the very back of the group, but soon they are just spots in the sea and we lose sight of them at the tip of the island. Then it's just the two of us heading across the open water towards Fejan.

After five minutes, we take a break from front crawl and do backstroke for a while. Then we switch to breaststroke. 'Where's Otto?' I call to Pearl.

'Can't talk,' she says. 'Concentrating.'

'It's weird,' I say, looking around. 'I can't see any support boats. Otto said he'd be next to us the whole way.' The sun beats down on my head, but the water is deliciously cool on my shoulders. 'Hey, Pearl,' I say.

'What?'

'We're in the middle of the sea!'

'Shh . . . don't want to think about it.'

'This is alright, isn't it?'

But Pearl doesn't answer because suddenly she screams, grabs me round my neck and tries to climb on my head. I go under the water and desperately try to kick my way up, all the time pushing her off. 'Something touched me!' she yells. 'Something touched me!'

'Let go,' I shout, but she just clings on even tighter. 'It's just a –' down I go again, but I splutter back to the surface and gasp – 'fish!'

'Gross, gross!' she cries as I finally manage to peel her from my shoulders. She swims in frantic circles, staring down into the water. 'It was massive. Can you see it? It sucked my toe!'

'It's a fish! *A fish*, Pearl.' I cough up the salty water I swallowed. 'You love fish, remember? It's a big Oy.'

We tread water and try to get our breathing under control. 'A fish?' she gasps. 'Yeah, OK. Yeah. Do you get sharks round here?'

'No.' I haven't got a clue.

'Right.' She takes a deep breath and pushes back her hair. Our feet paddle away under the water. 'Where are we?'

I look around. 'That's Stråla,' I say, pointing to the largest island, 'and we are supposed to be there.' I point ahead. 'So let's go.'

'Sorry,' she says, as we swim for the island.

'Don't worry about it.'

'It sucked my foot.'

'It was a fish.'

'A big fish.'

'Swim!'

When we get to Fejan, we scramble out of the sea and look around for the purple arrows. All the other contestants are long gone. 'I can't see any,' I say, running from tree to tree. 'Otto said the arrows would guide us to the kayaks. We must have come out on the wrong beach.' Pearl joins me, lifting up branches and peering under leaves. 'Come on. If we follow the path round the island, we'll find the kayaks.'

We run side by side, looking for the purple arrows or our kayak sitting on a beach. Somehow, we lose the path and have to scramble down the side of a slope. I trip and grab at a rock to stop myself falling. 'Wait for me,' I call to Pearl, as I try to get my balance.

And that's when I see it . . .

Wedged between two rocks is a flip-flop. A pink Miss Selfridge flip-flop. 'Oh my God . . .' I reach out and flick it to check it's really there.

'What?' Pearl turns round.

'I've done a bad thing,' I say, still staring at the flip-flop. 'We're not on Fejan, Pearl. We're on Vilda. Look.' I point out to sea. In the distance we can see another island, almost identical to Vilda. Moving away from it are a line of bright kayaks. 'That's Fejan.'

'No,' she says, shading her eyes.

'I'm sorry.'

'We're on the wrong island?' She drops to the ground. 'We're on the wrong *freakin'* island! We'll have to stay here until they come looking for us. We're not going to do it, Kat. She puts her head in her hands. I'm such an idiot. 'I actually thought we would!' I scramble down to her and put a hand on her shaking shoulders. 'Get off,' she says, twisting away from me.

'We *are* going to do it.' I push past her and half walk, half slide to the bottom of the hill. Then I run across the beach and keep going, straight into the sea.

'Kat, what are you doing?' Pearl runs after me.

Waves surge around my legs. 'Swimming to Fejan.'

'But I can't. I'm too tired.'

'You're not coming,' I say. 'I'm going on my own.' The water is up to my waist now. I keep wading forward. 'It's less than a kilometre away. I can do it easily. Then I'm going to get the kayak, come back here, pick you up and we are going to finish Tuff Troll.'

'Don't be stupid.' Pearl stands on a rock. 'It's too dangerous!'

Before Pearl can change my mind, I dive under the water and start swimming. Her insults drift across the water, increasing in rudeness the further I get from the shore. The last thing I hear her yell is, 'If you don't get your ass back here, I'm going to . . . ' Then her cries fade away and all I can hear is splashing water and the sound of my blood roaring in my ears.

Every twenty strokes, I look up and check I'm heading in the right direction. I'm not going to make the same mistake twice. It's harder than the swim to Vilda. Much harder. I'm not even halfway there, when my legs start to feel heavy in the water, but I don't think about it. I count my breaths, make my arms work and try, desperately, to find my zone.

I imagine myself from above, swimming in the middle of the ocean. A thing. A speck. I watch myself moving through the vast water and I remember when I was nine and Britta and I were allowed to swim alone to the bathing platform on the lake, my mum and dad watching from the shore. It was such an adventure. But I got tired, and I was scared that I couldn't make it, so Britta told me what French kissing was to distract me. She even did sound effects. Before I knew it, my fingers were touching the slippery wood and Britta was on the platform, hauling me up behind her. We stood side by side and waved at Mum and Dad. Right then, I knew that if I could swim to the platform, I could do anything!

And I was right. Fejan is getting closer, stroke by stroke. I *can* do anything! I force my arms and legs on and imagine I can see Britta's ponytail just ahead of me in the water. I might be a speck, but I'm a mighty speck! All around me, sun sparkles on the water, and I actually start to enjoy being all alone on the sea.

My zone is rudely interrupted by the roar of an engine. I look up and see one of the support boats heading towards me. Otto's at the wheel and he looks furious. He pulls the boat in an arc, stopping a few metres away. Waves wash over me and I abandon my stroke and tread water. 'Where the hell have you been?' Otto's pale and I can see sweat beading on his forehead. 'Where's Pearl?' his voice rises.

'On Vilda,' I say. 'She's fine.'

He lets out a huge sigh. 'Vilda? What's she doing on Vilda?'

'We swam to the wrong island.'

'What?' he says, slapping the wheel and almost laughing. 'Come on.' He reaches his arm out towards me. 'Get in.'

'No,' I say, paddling a few metres away from him.

'I said, *get in*. You broke the first rule of swimming, Kat: never swim alone. I have six boats out looking for you. Leo finished the race, then went straight back out. Everyone is worried sick.'

'I'm minutes away from Fejan,' I say, turning away. 'I can do it!' I start to swim towards the island.

'You made a mistake. Admit it and get in the bloody boat.'

'*I* made a mistake?' I yell over my shoulder. 'Follow the purple flags, you said. There'll be support boats *everywhere*!'

'There were, there are! But you and Pearl just disappeared.' He falls quiet for a moment. 'I suppose it might have been my fault. I was meant to stay with the last swimmers – you and Pearl – but I went ahead to check on the main group. Someone was in difficulty, so I sent Victor back to the end of the race, but he didn't realise you two were so far behind. When I took over, you had disappeared . . .'

'You lost us!'

'I know. But I didn't think you would swim to the *wrong* island.' I hear Otto speaking into his walkie-talkie and then the boat splutters into life.

'I'm not getting in the boat, Otto.' I keep swimming.

'No, I can see that, but I'm not letting you out of my sight. Do you want water?'

'No. You might try and drag me on board.'

'Bloody stupid girl.'

Twenty painful, exhausting minutes later, I crawl on to a flat grey rock and flop on my back. I was doggy-paddling by the end. 'You OK?' Otto shouts from the boat.

'Everything . . . wobbly,' I whisper.

'Catch.'

I look up just in time to see a bottle of water flying towards me. Unfortunately, I'm too weak to move out of the way and it smashes into my face. I grab hold of it before it rolls off the rock and lie back, holding the ice-cold bottle against my cheek. 'Sorry,' says Otto. 'There's more water in your kayak. I'm going to check on Pearl. But I'll be back!' I sit up and watch as he turns the boat around and shoots off towards Vilda, leaving a trail of white foam.

I drag myself to my feet, unscrew the bottle and take a sip of the most delicious water I've ever tasted in my life. Then I find the first purple arrow and plod into the woods. I force my legs to move faster until I'm almost, almost, jogging. More staggering, really. 'Come on, legs,' I say desperately. 'Don't stop working. In a minute, you'll be resting in a kayak and it's all going to be down to the arms.' I'm talking to my legs. Maybe I'm dehydrated. 'Sorry, arms,' I add, then I have a big drink of water before I start talking to any other body part.

Otto catches up with me as I leave Fejan. All the way to Vilda, he follows me in the speedboat, yelling lots of useful advice. I keep telling him to go away, but he ignores me. Really, I'm pleased he's here. *Wild Kat* is a heavy kayak built for two, and my arms and legs are barely working. Towards the end of training, Pearl and I were averaging one kilometre in twenty minutes. When I finally see Pearl standing on the beach of Vilda, a colourful tie-died figure, hair covered in silver beads and face smeared with blue, red and white face paint, I've been kayaking for over forty minutes.

'Go Kat!' she yells, jumping up and down. 'You nutter! You actually did it!' She wades into the sea and hauls herself into the front of the kayak. 'Let's finish this race.' Pearl grabs her paddle, drags it through the water and pulls us round and back out to sea.

The pain in my shoulders eases and I feel a mad new strength. 'Otto,' I say. 'You can go back to Stråla now. Honestly. We'll be fine.'

'I know,' he says. 'Girls. Do you want these?' He holds up two Plopp bars.

'Did the others have one?'

281

'No. I got them for emergencies.'

'We're fine,' I say. 'We're finishing the race just like everyone else. We just did an extra tough version of it.'

Otto shrugs. 'See you back at Stråla,' he says, then he revs the engine and zooms away.

'I badly want a Plopp,' says Pearl.

The journey to Stråla is painful, but strangely chilled out. We know the worst is over now. Luckily, Pearl is pumped and does most of the work. 'Say goodbye to Reception Rock,' she says as we paddle past it.

'Bye, Rock,' I say, remembering how tired I got swimming out to it the first time. Now the distance looks tiny.

'When we get in, I bet they've all gone home,' says Pearl. 'When do you think the others finished?'

'About two hours ago?'

'And how long has it taken us?'

'Over three hours.'

'That's funny,' says Pearl, and she starts to laugh. 'Three hours! We've definitely broken a Tuff Troll record.'

'But we did it,' I say. 'We've definitely got a story to tell.'

'Thanks to *Wild Kat*.'

I give the kayak a pat. 'She may be battered and leak a bit, but she got us back safely.'

Pearl turns round and laughs. 'I mean you, you idiot. I knew you could do it.'

'Thanks,' I say, but Pearl's already turned away. We go on in silence, past our cottage, heading for the cafe and harbour. The evening light is soft and golden and Pearl's hair beads shine in the low sun. Our paddles dip in and out of the water and I can't see where the milky sea ends and the pale sky begins.

'My bum is going to ache on the plane tomorrow,' I say as we round the rocks by the cafe.

'Look,' says Pearl. Floating past our kayak is a paper lantern and inside a candle flickers. 'Otto said he had lanterns to light when it got dark. Someone's done one early.'

'There's another one,' I say. We paddle on, the two lanterns bumping against the side of our kayak. We pass the tip of the island and suddenly we are gliding through a sea of paper lanterns.

'No one's gone home,' Pearl whispers.

I look up. The harbour and cafe are lined with people. As soon as they see us, they start to cheer and call out to us, encouraging us home. I see Frida and Nils at the end of the jetty, and jumping up and down on our rock are Sören and Nanna. I scan the crowd. All the other contestants are there too, changed and showered, and wearing Tuff Troll medals. I even spot numbers seven and eight wearing brand new 'I ♥ Stråla' hoodies. Peeta and Leo are nowhere to be seen.

'They lit the lanterns for us,' says Pearl.

'Are you *crying*?' I ask.

'*Shut up!* It's your splashy paddling. See, I've got splashes on my clothes.'

'And your cheeks.'

'It's just so pretty,' she says, 'like a fairy tale.'

We glide through the glowing lanterns and as we reach the pier, arms reach down and haul us out of the kayak and on to dry land. Otto appears in front of us.

'Welcome home, our very Tuff Trolls.' He places a gold medal round my sunburnt neck and I smile. I'm too tired to talk. 'You deserve that,' he says. 'A two-kilometre sea swim is quite an achievement.' Hands clap me on the back, someone presses a bottle of water into my hand and a towel is draped over my shoulders. Otto gives me my Plopp.

He turns to Pearl. 'This is for you.' He struggles to get her medal over her beads, so she takes over, forcing it over her wild hair and round her neck. Next, Otto gets a sheet of stickers out of his pocket, peels off a small red star and sticks it on her medal.

'That makes forty,' she says, smoothing down each point. Otto hands her a roll-up cigarette, which she tucks behind her ear. 'Thanks,' she murmurs, staring at the star.

'Now, I need to get this party started,' says Otto, pushing his way through the crowd.

Nanna finds us and drags us into the cafe just as Otto's mike bursts into life. '*Är du redo att rocka?*' he shouts, then dance music blasts across the *mötesplats* followed by Otto growling, 'Seckseee deescow!'

It's the best Disco Otto ever.

Pearl and I binge on fries and ice cream, and as the sun goes down, we dance with Nanna to ABBA. Even though I'm still wearing my spotty shorts and my nose is peeling, I feel just right. When Otto puts on 'Happyland', Nanna and Pearl go crazy, but I decide to sit it out. As I keep reminding everyone, I swam a very long way today. I sit with my back against our rock and watch as Otto gets the crowd doing the sprinkler. Then I see Peeta weaving through the dancers, ducking to avoid all the jiggling elbows.

It's like a rerun of the day she arrived on the island, only this time it's me she's walking towards, and me that she's smiling at. I have to stop myself from looking behind me.

'*Hej*, Kat,' she says. Yep. Definitely me.

'*Hej*.' I look up at her. She's wearing a strappy dress and the very last rays of sun shine on her golden hair and Tuff Troll medal. 'You look resplendent!' I say.

'Thanks.' She says this uncertainly and twirls a bottle of Fanta round in her hands.

'You do. I mean it. I like your dress.'

After a moment's hesitation, she sits down opposite me. 'You got back OK?'

'Would you believe that we swam to the wrong island?'

'Really?' She laughs, but for once it's not a mean laugh. For a while, we sit and watch Pearl trying to teach Nanna to moonwalk, but Nanna keeps getting the giggles and eventually they give up. Peeta says, 'You're going home tomorrow, right?'

'All the way back to England.'

'That's what I thought.' She pauses then says, 'Did you know Leo and me split up?' She glances across at me, still twisting her bottle, then quickly carries on. 'It was ages ago, the day after I arrived here, and I didn't take it very well. My mum and dad hate each other at the moment and Leo makes me feel calm, you know?'

'I guess,' I say. Leo's made me feel a lot of things this summer, but then I remember when I jumped off the cliff into the pool, how he looked up at me and smiled. I nod. 'I know what you mean.'

'I told him that I wasn't going to leave Stråla. I thought I could change his mind just by being around.' She laughs and shakes her head. 'Anyway, it didn't work and I'm going tomorrow too. I wanted to say goodbye and to say sorry if I've been a bit crazy, you see . . . I was jealous of you.'

The sun has gone now and our corner of the terrace is in shadow, the only light coming from little candles that flicker in jars. I look at Peeta. She's hugging her knees. 'Because Leo took me kayaking?' I ask.

'A little, but really it was seeing you with your friends. You've all had so much fun together.' I look across at the dancefloor. Pearl and Nanna are slow dancing with Sören. I don't think Sören wants to be there. He's definitely trying to escape.

'I don't have many friends,' Peeta says. 'Leo was one of them, but I messed that up.' I think about the times Nanna, Pearl and I went Fun Running round the island, and how often we saw Peeta watching us. We never asked her to join in.

'So, I've got to go and pack,' she says, getting up. I stand up too, wincing as my poor bum muscles are forced into action. 'Tomorrow I'm going to go home and hang out with Annika, my best friend. Hopefully, when Leo gets back, we can be friends again.'

We face each other, and I'm not sure what to say. I realise I don't really want to say goodbye. 'Maybe we'll meet up again, here on Stråla.'

'Maybe . . . I could bring Annika,' she says.

'Dance at Disco Otto . . .'

'. . . Compete in Tuff Troll. I'll have to get her training with me.' She steps round the rock and hugs me. '*Hej då*, Kat.'

'*Hej då*,' I say. Then she lets go, waves and walks through the dancers, her hair floating out behind her.

Nanna calls me over. Otto has put on 'I Need a Hero' and as far as she's concerned, this is our song. 'Come and dance!'

I shake my head. 'My legs are killing me.' But this isn't a good enough excuse. She walks over and drags me on to the dancefloor where Pearl is waiting for us.

TWENTY

Later, I leave Nanna and Pearl dancing and walk to the end of the pier. I sit down, letting my bare feet dangle in the water, and I stare across the sea at the full moon. A silver path stretches from my toes to the horizon. I feel like I could step out on to it. I nudge a lantern away with my toe.

'They're eco-lanterns.' I look round. Leo's standing behind me. He smiles uncertainly. 'They don't have wire so they should biodegrade, but I'm still not sure they're safe . . .' He trails off. 'Kat,' he says, stepping closer. 'If I sit next to you, will you jump in the sea?'

'No.' I laugh. 'I'm so tired I wouldn't be able to get out again.' He sits down and even though we aren't touching, somehow I can feel the warmth of his shoulders. 'Where've you been?' I say, giving him a small nudge.

'I had to do a lot of packing up for Otto. I'm basically his slave for the summer.' He pauses. 'Kat, I was so worried when you went missing.'

'Thank you for looking for us,' I say.

'I just kept telling myself you'd both be OK because I know how well you can swim. I thought about when we went to Vilda –'

'When I was being such an airhead? Screaming at the tiniest drop of water and desperate to work on my tan?' I glance across at him and smile. I'm not even annoyed when I say this.

He shakes his head. 'That's not what I thought.'

'Then why did you say those things?' Before I go home, I want to understand everything.

'Because I panicked and tried to hide the truth from Peeta. I thought, just by seeing us together, Peeta would know.'

'Know what?'

Leo turns to look at me, but I stare at the sea. I don't want to say or do anything because that precious feeling between the two of us that began on Vilda is coming back and it feels so wonderful it's like being bathed in sunlight, except it's moonlight shining down on us. Leo slips his hand into mine. Our hands fit together perfectly. 'Kat, I have liked you since the first moment I met you.'

'Since the naked Little Frog dance?' I ask. Then I go, '*Ack ack*,' which is essentially 'ribbit, ribbit' in Swedish, and is a crazy thing to say when you have just been told the best news.

He laughs. 'It was a memorable moment.' He squeezes my hand. 'Hey,' he says, 'are you going to look at me.' I turn and face him. 'Still not going to jump into the sea?' I shake my head. 'Because there's something important I need to say, something I should have said on the roof of Otto's cabin.' He doesn't take his eyes off me. 'I'm sorry I didn't tell you I had a girlfriend and

I'm sorry I said those things about you. You're not *blåst*. You're the opposite of *blåst*. You're *rolig ...* *modig.*' *Funny, brave.* He looks at me to check I understand. 'That day . . .' He holds my hand a little tighter. '*Det betydde allt för mig.*' *It meant everything to me.*

'*Mig också,*' I say. *Me too.* Now I'm blushing in the darkness, so I rest my head against him and he puts his arm around me. I thought everything between us had disappeared, just like the sparkling phosphorescence, but now it's come back. And it's still magical. Resting against Leo feels even better than I imagined and, for a minute, I let myself enjoy the warmth of his chest and being held by him.

Even though it is amazing to hear him say these things, I wonder how Peeta would feel if she could see us now. I know exactly how she'd feel. 'You know,' I say, 'tonight Peeta told me that you broke up ages ago.'

'I tried to tell you, but you kept throwing buckets at me . . . or running away.'

'Hey, you trod on my cinnamon bun.'

'OK, but now, Kat, I *don't* have a girlfriend, and right now you are here and I am here, and so are the stars. Otto's playing "Guantanamera" again, and we've even got *lanterns*!'

He's right. It is the moment I was dreaming about . . . before I met Peeta. And it would be so easy to reach up and kiss him. I look out to sea and I remember when I was swimming alone to Fejan, just a speck in the ocean.

Suddenly, I know what I have to do. I force myself to lift my head off his shoulder and sit up.

'Do you know,' I say, 'doing this race today, finishing it, is the best thing I have *ever* done. If I hadn't met you, if we hadn't gone to Vilda and you hadn't believed I could jump off that cliff, I might never have done it. I'm even going to do a race with my family, Cliff Hanger, and all because you reminded me how brave I can be. But I can't stop thinking about Peeta right now, and I don't want my last memory of Strâla to be kissing you, Peeta's ex-boyfriend, and then going home and never seeing you again.'

295

'Why wouldn't we see each other again?'

I laugh. 'Because you'll have forgotten about me in a few weeks and we live eight hundred miles away from each other.'

'Maybe I'm never going to forget you. Maybe I like you so much that eight hundred miles is nothing. Next summer, you could come back here. We can kayak all over the archipelago and stay on a different island every night. We could have a whole summer of Vildas!'

'My dad would love that!'

'He could come too, and your mum, and Britta. We could race them from island to island.' I look at his kind brown eyes and shake my head. 'So this is it?' He looks slightly amazed.

I nod. 'Goodbye, Leo,' I say and I stand up. I pull him to his feet and we hug. We probably hug for a bit too long and usually when I hug someone I don't use my entire body, or rest my head on the other person's shoulder, or smell them . . . and then try and pin down the smell because it's the best smell in the world and I never want to forget it.

'Goodbye, Kat,' Leo says into my hair. It's hard to stop an amazing hug, but Pearl helps.

'Phosphorescence,' she yells, grabbing me by the arm and pulling me away. 'Back at the cottage. Frida just told me. Let's go.' She pulls me down the pier. 'Nice knowing you, Leo!' she calls, and I let her drag me away from Leo and somehow I don't look back.

TWENTY-ONE

'Never forget me!' yells Nanna. She's come to the dock to see us off and she's wearing a batman onesie. As she jumps up and down her cape flies out behind her.

Our boat moves away from the dock and starts to pick up speed. Pearl and I hold on to the rail and water sprays into our faces. 'We won't, you freak!' shouts Pearl.

All I can do is wave. Last night, I was on a Tuff Troll high. Pearl and I splashed around in phosphorescence then stayed up late chatting to Frida and finishing our packing; leaving didn't seem real. Later, when I lay in bed, I couldn't sleep, even though I was exhausted. The engine roars as the boat bumps over a wave. Nanna is tiny now, but I don't take my eyes off her or the dock. The further we get from Stråla, the sadder I feel until I realise, in a panic, that this is it. I've left Leo behind.

'Pearl,' I say, grabbing her arm. 'I think I made a terrible mistake.'

'Yep. You should have snogged him.'

'But if I had, wouldn't I feel even worse now?'

Pearl shrugs. 'It's what I'd have done. Do you want a Lakrisal?' She holds out the packet to me. 'Take all of them,' she says. 'I've got loads in my bag. I'm going to find Frida.'

Even though Lakrisal taste like salty medicine, I peel back the silver paper and put one in my mouth. When I look up, I can't see Nanna, and Stråla is just a lump of rocks and trees, one of many islands scattered across the archipelago. My chest aches and I suck the sweet. *I did the right thing*, I tell myself, again and again, until Stråla is a dot on the horizon. And then, in a flash of sunlight, it disappears.

★

Travelling across Stockholm on no sleep and a semi-broken heart is tiring. Somehow, Frida manages to get us to the airport on time, even though Pearl has a major tantrum when she discovers that we can't go to the ABBA museum.

'Time to say goodbye,' Frida says. We've just shared a pizza and now Pearl and I need to go through security. Frida gives me the biggest hug and I bury my face in her wild hair. She smells of Stråla – of salt and coconut suntan lotion. Even Pearl allows herself to be hugged and, at the last minute, she gives Frida the briefest of squeezes. 'I made you these,' says Frida. She puts her hand in her pocket and pulls out two tangled necklaces. She takes one and hands it to me. 'Here's yours, Pearl.'

The necklaces are round silver pendants, beaten flat. Mine looks like it's been broken in half and it has squiggly black lines on it. 'Put them together!' Frida is excited. I hold my necklace next to Pearl's. They fit perfectly. The squiggly lines come together to make a kayak. Sitting in the kayak are two girls, hair streaming behind them, their paddles held high above their heads.

Pearl runs her fingers over the picture. 'It's us,' she says, smiling. Then she puts her necklace on and so do I.

'Thank you,' I say to Frida, rubbing the smooth metal between my fingers. Frida gives me one last hug then pushes us forward.

Soon, we're sitting in the departure lounge waiting for our plane to board. 'Baby Kex?' asks Pearl. She's just used up the last of her kronor in the snack shop and discovered Kex come in handy-size packs. I shake my head. It might be the lack of sleep, but suddenly I feel sick. Our flight is called and all around us people pick up their bags and form a queue. Usually, I'd be right at the front. I hate being the last one on to a plane, but I stay in my seat, my legs tucked under me, staring at the door that leads into the departure lounge.

When there are only a handful of passengers waiting

to get on the plane, I'm still in my seat. 'Come on,' says Pearl. 'What are you waiting for?'

'Nothing,' I say, finally accepting that Leo isn't going to rush in and sweep me off my feet. I stand up and grab my bag. 'Let's go home.'

Pearl is quiet on the flight, but that suits me. I rest my head against the window and do some cloud spotting. Soon, I see neat squares of green fields below me, curving roads and matchbox houses. We're back. The nose of the plane tilts down and the seatbelt light comes on. As we're bumping along the runway, lurching from side to side, I realise that I don't feel scared; I didn't even feel scared when we took off.

After collecting our bags, we wander in a daze through a maze of corridors, following the 'Exit' signs.

'I can't wait to have a shower,' Pearl says. 'I think I've still got some phosphorescence stuck in my hair.'

'I'm going to have a bath, with bubbles,' I say, 'and then I'm going to eat sliced white bread with Marmite.' We turn a corner into another endless corridor. 'And

I'm getting some big fat chips, not fries, and for breakfast I'm having Weetabix.'

'Weetabix! I'd forgotten about Weetabix,' says Pearl. 'Hang on. Toilets. I'm desperate. I never go on planes in case my bum gets sucked out of the hole.'

I follow her in. 'I don't think that can happen.'

'Yes it can,' she says, going into a cubicle. 'I saw it on YouTube.'

While I wait with our bags, I glance in the mirror. My hair is tangled and salty stiff and my nose is pink. Freckles are scattered across my cheeks and I've got a yellow bruise on my cheek where the bottle of water hit me. I peer closer. Is that blood? I rub at a mark on my chin. It comes off. It was just a bit of face paint. All round my hairline is a faint blue smudge: more face paint.

'C'mon, Wild Kat,' says Pearl, taking her case and pushing open the door. 'You look gorgeous.'

We walk down one more corridor, through double doors, then find ourselves in the arrivals hall. All round us, people are being swept into welcoming arms. I scan the crowd until I spot Mum and Dad. 'Mum!' I shout, dragging my suitcase towards them.

'Kat?' She peers at me. 'Is that you?' Then I see two girls standing behind her. One has a cloud of brown curls, the other is wearing a boob hat. Bea and Betty! I abandon my case and run, throwing myself into a big group hug. There's a lot of jumping and screaming, and a little bit of crying. Dad always gets emotional at airports. 'What's Frida done to you?' asks Mum, laughing and smoothing my hair down.

'You look awesome,' says Betty, 'like you've been in a fight. Is that a scar?'

I laugh and shake my head. 'Just a bruise,' I say. 'A bottle of water hit me on the cheek.'

'No, on your forehead.'

'Oh, maybe!' I touch my head, remembering when Leo put a plaster there.

'Did you have a good time, Kat?' asks Bea, taking my hand. I look down at my fingers, which are rough and covered in blisters from paddling the kayak. A thousand memories flash through my mind. I think about Nanna's pink high-tops and blonde curls, the sloping ceilings in our attic room, 'Guantanamera', cinnamon buns and golden sunsets. And I think about a boy.

I nod, but I can't say anything. I look around for Pearl. She's rescued my suitcase and is sitting on it. She scowls at me and sticks Otto's unlit roll-up in her mouth.

'For God's sake, Kat,' says Dad, peering down at my feet. 'Where are your shoes?'

TWENTY-TWO

'Have you seen Mum and Dad?' I ask. Britta and I are lying on our stomachs in thick mud. We can't stand up – we're trapped under a net.

Britta shakes her head. 'I think we lost them at the logs.'

'Coming through!' shouts a man wearing a bandana. He wriggles between us. Britta and I follow him, crawling forward on our elbows. The mud is icy and drizzle is falling on us. Britta gets out first and reaches back for me. I grab hold of her hand, she pulls me out and we follow the crowd running along the narrow track.

We're in Dorset, competing in Cliff Hanger. We're three kilometres in and have twenty-six 'hard-core obstacles' to go. I don't think I've ever seen Dad happier than he was at the start line. 'I'm racing with my three girls,' he had said, gathering us to him. 'What a story!'

'What's next?' I ask as Britta and I stumble along the path, the sea roaring somewhere below us.

'Steps,' gasps Britta.

'Steps? That's not a badass obstacle!' I look ahead and see a steep cliff with steps cut into the rock. 'Oh. That's a lot of steps. We're running up them?'

'All eighty-three of them,' says Britta. She's about to start, then she steps to one side. 'You go first.'

And I do run up the steps, not jog, *run*. Below me, the sea is grey and waves smash against the cliff. It's November, and Stråla's sparkling blue sea is a distant memory.

I'm in Year Eleven now. I still hang out with Betty and Bea, go shopping with Mum and straighten my hair before school. But some things have changed. A few times a week, I go running, sometimes on my own and sometimes with Britta. Dad got me a mountain bike for my birthday and we've been cycling together. On Sunday, he took me out in the woods. As we crossed the park I saw Pearl sitting on the climbing frame with her friends. She was smoking and all the beads had come out of her hair. When she saw me, she stood up, stuck her fag in her mouth and did the Ladybird wave. That's when I noticed she was wearing a T-shirt that said, 'I Pooped Today!' I couldn't see if she had her necklace on, but I was wearing mine.

Sometimes, for a special treat, I put on ABBA, lie on my bed and suck a Lakrisal. Then I shut my eyes, taste liquorice and salt, and think about Leo. It feels like a wonderful dream that's slipping away from me. I've got one Lakrisal left.

'C'mon!' Britta is pushing my bum. I look up. Only a few more steps to go. I force myself on. 'What can you see?' she shouts.

'Tyres! We've got to run over tyres.'

'I love tyres,' says Britta. 'They're the best!' She's not joking. We stumble over the tyres, trying to keep our knees high, and I think about Nanna running like a horse. Ahead of us is a muddy ditch full of water that we are expected to wade through.

We slither down the bank and plunge into the ditch. The water's freezing and comes up to my chest. I pull an ice cube out of my vest. Now that's just mean! All around us, people push and shove as they try to move forward. I grab hold of Britta's vest to stop myself from falling over.

As we're scrambling out at the other end, a woman runs past me, bumping into my back. I lose my footing, my fingers slip off Britta and I fall down in the mud. Britta doesn't notice and keeps going. I try to get up, but someone treads on my hair and my face slaps down again. I laugh, wipe the mud out of my eyes and rest on my elbows, waiting until I've got my breath back.

Suddenly, two hands are round my shoulders, pulling me up out of the mud and holding me steady. I turn round to see who has rescued me. It's a boy. A boy with messy brown hair, brown eyes and a face that I love and just can't forget, even when it's covered in mud.

'Leo?' I rest my hands on his chest. I feel his heart beating under my fingers. 'What are you doing here?'

His hands tighten round me, like he doesn't want me to run away. 'I just came to tell you . . .' He pauses, trying to get his breath back.

'What?' We are being bumped on all sides as people stagger out of the ditch.

'That I still like you.' He smiles and instantly I'm bathed in Stråla sunshine. 'I *eight hundred miles* like you.'

I laugh, stepping closer to him. 'Did you rehearse that?'

'It was a long journey. I had a lot of time to think about what I wanted to say.'

'How did you find me?'

'You told me you were doing this race and I just hoped I'd bump into you . . . and I have.'

'What are you going to do now you've bumped into me?'

He looks embarrassed, like he hasn't thought that far ahead. 'I'm going to finish the race, with you, and then I thought we could have a coffee, maybe some chocolate – I've brought Plopp and Kex – and talk for a bit. I've actually got nowhere to sleep tonight. Can I stay at your house?'

I nod. 'But you've forgotten the most important thing you've got to do.'

'What?' he says, looking worried.

'This.' I move closer, ignoring the muddy, sweaty people who push past us, and I reach up and hold his face in my hands. Rain starts to fall and in the distance there's a rumble of thunder, but I barely notice because now I'm kissing Leo and it's even more magical than phosphorescence. Leo wraps his arms round me and our race numbers become tangled. His heart beats close to mine. The rain gets heavier, but we don't care, because we've found each other at last.

'Kat?' Britta's shocked voice makes me let go of Leo and spin round. 'What are you doing?'

'This is Leo,' I say, 'and he's joining our team.'

'If that's OK,' he says.

'What's next?' I ask Britta.

'A big slippery wall we have to get over,' she says, still staring at Leo, wide-eyed. 'We'll need to climb on someone's shoulders.'

'You turned up at just the right moment,' I tell Leo. Then I pull him up the bank and we join Britta running along the cliff path. A gust of wind slams into us. I glance sideways, looking at Leo as he runs beside me in his mud-streaked vest. Rain falls down the back of my top and my fingers and toes are numb from the cold. I smile and shake my head.

'What?' he says, laughing.

'Nothing,' I say . . . As if I'm going to tell him that he just hit ten out of ten.

LOOK OUT FOR **PEARL'S** STORY OF

MUSIC
FRENEMiES
AND TROPICAL FISH

STAR
STRUCK

COMiNG SPRING 2016

MEET THE OTHER LADYBIRDS!

FLIRTY DANCING

BEA HAS ENTERED A TV DANCE COMPETITION. BUT HER PARTNER TURNS OUT TO BE THE UNBELIEVABLY HOT BOYFRIEND OF THE MEANEST GIRL IN SCHOOL!

LOVE BOMB

BETTY KNOWS NOTHING ABOUT BOYS AND HER ONLY PASSIONATE KISS WAS WITH A CAT. SO WHEN THE GORGEOUS TOBY EXPLODES INTO HER LIFE SHE NEEDS HELP!